EDGAR; OR, THE PHANTOM OF THE CASTLE

Gothic Classics

Edgar;

or, the

Phantom of the Castle

by

Richard Sickelmore

Edited by James D. Jenkins

"—————————Foul deeds will rise,
Though all the earth o'erwhelm them, to men's eyes."

VALANCOURT BOOKS
CHICAGO

Edgar; or, the Phantom of the Castle
First published 1798
First Valancourt Books edition, August 2005

ISBN 0-9766048-9-2
Library of Congress Control Number: 2005903941

Published by Valancourt Books, Chicago, Illinois
Printed in the United States of America

CONTENTS

CONTENTS

INTRODUCTION

Richard Sickelmore was born around 1780 at Brighton.[1] His father, Richard Sickelmore, Sr., was a local printer and the author of several works on the history and topography of Brighton and must have encouraged young Richard in his literary pursuits. As a young man, Sickelmore began his writing career as a playwright, composing some pieces which were printed and acted at his native Brighton.

Sickelmore turned to novel writing with *Edgar; or, the Phantom of the Castle*, which was published by William Lane's Minerva Press in 1798 to generally favourable reviews. Sickelmore, in his preface to *Edgar*, acknowledges its imperfections, but seeks to excuse himself by stating that his only purpose in writing the book was to amuse himself during a dreary vacation in Brighton, and to earn some money to benefit his family. But despite the novel's shortcomings, it was well received by a public still enamoured of Gothic romances in the style of Ann Radcliffe.

Sickelmore followed *Edgar* with another Minerva Press romance, *Mary-Jane* (1800), of which Frederick S. Frank writes, "Behind the deceptively innocuous title, *Mary-Jane* is an outrageously horrid adventure sometimes rising (or

---

[1] The dates of Richard Sickelmore's birth and death are unknown. His first play was published in 1797 and his first novel in 1798, and it may be assumed that he authored these first works at around age eighteen or nineteen—the same age at which Francis Lathom, Percy Bysshe Shelley, and M. G. Lewis published their first Gothic novels—which would put his date of birth at around 1780. His date of death is more difficult to approximate, but he is listed as the printer on the title page of a number of books through at least the 1840s and must have died sometime around the middle of the 19th century.

sinking) to the degree of loathsome detail and cadaverous exhibitionism associated with [...] Monk Lewis." The novel was exceedingly popular, and cemented Sickelmore's status as one of the foremost of the Minerva Press Gothic novelists.

His next major novel, *Rashleigh Abbey; or, the Ruin on the Rock* (1805) was favourably reviewed by *The Literary Journal* of December, 1805, which speaks to the novel's quality, since by 1805 the popularity of the Gothic romance was already in decline, and the critics, who had never been particularly indulgent towards the Gothic as a genre, were by that time even less so. By the time *Rashleigh Abbey* was published, Sickelmore was a widely-read novelist and must have moved in literary circles, as suggested in his dedication of the novel to the Lady Charlotte Lennox, by whose efforts, Sickelmore writes, "this Work [...] will find its way into the most polished circles of life."

Sickelmore's next novel, *Osrick: or, Modern Horrors* (1809), is considered by Montague Summers and Frederick Frank to be his most important work. Like *Rashleigh Abbey*, it bears a dedication to a noble female patron, this time, Countess Craven,[2] whom Sickelmore somewhat disingenuously begs pardon for his "inconsiderable work" and his own "insignificance." Unlike his previous efforts, however, *Osrick* is a radically experimental novel. The book is not divided in chapters, but rather is told in a sort of journalistic prose with sensationalized headlines occurring periodically throughout the story, with such attention-grabbers as "*A PICTURE OF HUMAN MISERY*", "*A FRIGHTFUL ABYSS,*" and "*A*

---

[2] Countess Craven, née Louisa Brunton, was an actress famed for her beauty, and well known at the time as a connoisseur of literature.

SPECTRE," and with the conversations frequently presented in dramatic dialogue, with speech-prefixes, as in a play.

After 1809, Sickelmore stopped publishing novels and plays. The reason for this is unknown, but most likely, he had enjoyed such financial success from his novels that he no longer needed to write for money and could turn to other pursuits which he found more interesting. During the latter part of his life, Sickelmore seems to have devoted the bulk of his time and effort to the management of the printing and publishing company founded by his father, which remained an important publishing house in Brighton through at least the 1840s.

Little is known about Sickelmore's life, besides what we can learn from his literary output. A contemporary source, *Biographia Dramatica* (1812) gives us a brief, largely unflattering account of Sickelmore, which provides some details:

SICKLEMORE, R. A person still living at Brighton, who has the merit of having raised himself from a mechanic line of life by his pen, as balnean purveyor of chit-chat news for the London papers; which articles being invariably larded with the epithet pedestrian and equestrian, as well as being written in a sort of stilted prose, have obtained him the name of *Apollo on Horseback.* He is, however, a very worthy character; and, besides some rhymes, of which one may say,

   On peut etre honnete homme, et faire mal des vers,[3] has contributed several pieces of *novel* goods to the light summer manufactory of Lane and Co.

---

[3] One may be a perfect gentleman, and write bad verses. (The quotation is from Molière's *Le Misanthrope*).

[New readers may wish to return to the remainder of this introduction after completing the novel, as it discusses some elements of the plot.]

One of the first observations the reader of *Edgar; or, the Phantom of the Castle* will make is, that there is no actual phantom at any point in the novel, nor is there any particularly important castle. The only mention of a phantom at all in the novel is when Edgar dons his murdered father's armour and is mistaken by the conscience-stricken evildoers for his ghost.[4] And although there certainly is a castle mentioned in the novel, most of the important events occur not at the castle, but in a ruined priory. However, lurid titles were often affixed to fairly humdrum-sounding Gothics to increase sales. Judging from the titles of Sickelmore's other early novels (*Agnes and Leonora*, *Mary-Jane*, and *Raymond*), the author probably originally named the book simply "*Edgar*"; the subtitle "*Phantom of the Castle*" was most likely added by the publisher to ensure that readers would know that the book was a Gothic romance and not a "serious" novel.[5]

Edgar is plainly the work of a talented, but youthful writer, and bears the clear signs of its principal influences, Horace Walpole's *The Castle of Otranto* (1764), the romances of Ann Radcliffe, and the tragedies of Shakespeare.

---

[4] Strangely, in Frederick Frank's *The First Gothics*, Frank's discussion of the plot of *Edgar; or, the Phantom of the Castle* involves a phantom who reveals the secrets of the murder of Edgar's father and demands vengeance, but as the reader will see, these events do not take place in this novel.

[5] The novel was translated into French in 1800 as *Edgar: ou le Pouvoir du remords* (*Edgar: or the Power of Remorse*), which is certainly a much more apt title, given the book's plot.

The novel is essentially a gothicized retelling of the *Hamlet* tale, which, in itself, would not make it unique; this theme was exceedingly common in both Gothic novels and chapbooks of the period. However, Sickelmore's excellent imitation of Radcliffe's techniques of "sublime terror" and his uncommonly successful use of the gloomy and almost surreal atmosphere of *The Castle of Otranto*, render it one of the best Gothics of this style.

As the contemporary critics remarked,[6] Sickelmore displays a masterful command of Radcliffe's method of evoking terror. His descriptions of the ruined abbey and the raging storm bear clear marks of Radcliffe's influence, as do his careful rational explanations of any circumstance that might have appeared supernatural. However, Sickelmore does depart at times from Radcliffe's school of terror in favour of elements of "Monk" Lewis's mode of horror. The grotesque description of the villain Bernardine and the fairly gruesome details of several murders perpetrated during the tale are worthy of Lewis himself. In the end, however, Sickelmore is careful not to stray too far down the paths of horror, preferring to confine himself to a story which, as he says in his preface, will not "convey a wrong idea to the head, or a corrupt wish to the heart."

But if Sickelmore was influenced by the styles of Radcliffe and, to a lesser extent, Lewis, he is mostly indebted to Shakespeare for his plot. In both Shakespeare's *Hamlet* and Sickelmore's *Edgar*, the noble father of the young prince is murdered by a treacherous uncle, who then resolves on the destruction of the son to insure his continued power; similarly, in both works, the young man is described as an

---

[6] The full text of the contemporary reviews is included in this book as an appendix.

irresolute and undetermined youth who struggles with his duty to avenge his father. However, it is not the similarities between the two stories which are instructive, but the differences. Interestingly, Sickelmore gothicizes several elements of the Hamlet story, replacing the lovesick and tragic Ophelia with the hideous and unsympathetic Lucretia (and then crushing her to death virtually at random, in true *Otranto* style), and substituting murderous banditti for the more subtle assassins Rosencrantz and Guildenstern in Shakespeare's story. But the most intriguing departure Sickelmore makes from Shakespeare's original is the absence of the vengeful ghost who, in *Hamlet*, appears to his son to demand retribution. Sickelmore's decision to omit the ghost and substitute for its revelatory role the second-hand accounts of Edgar's friend Bardolph and Edgar's discovery of his murdered father's armour, is obviously owing to the influence of Ann Radcliffe, who eschewed the use of supernatural phenomena in her works.

However, it is to be regretted that Sickelmore's titular phantom does not figure more prominently in the story. As with many of the works written in imitation of Mrs. Radcliffe, *Edgar; or, the Phantom of the Castle* suffers from an anticlimactic ending, when all the terror and horror so expertly built up over the novel's two volumes is dissipated by a pat explanation of all the strange events leading up to the conclusion. Still more frustrating is the unsatisfying demise of the scheming Sir Armine and his minion Bernardine, who despite their long years of evil misdeeds, pass away into the next life without bloodshed, repenting their wrongs and hoping for happiness in the next life. Sickelmore probably included the moralistic ending to appease contemporary critics, who tended to praise a novel with a good moral, while decrying works like Lewis's *The Monk* as blasphemous and immoral, but today's readers will likely find the ending disappointing.

Whatever may be its shortcomings, *Edgar; or, the Phantom of the Castle* is an example of one of the better minor Gothic novels written in the late 1790s, and the influence of this book and Sickelmore's later works can be felt throughout later Gothic novels. While the story's moral may be that of an earlier time, the overall enjoyability of the tale has not diminished; and although many Gothic novelists copied incidents from Walpole and Radcliffe, few were as adept as Sickelmore at evoking Walpole's atmospheric gloom or Radcliffe's pleasing terror.

This novel has languished in obscurity for two centuries and has not seen reprinting since its initial publication in 1798. Valancourt Books is pleased to correct this oversight by presenting to a new generation of Gothic readers and scholars this edition of *Edgar; or, the Phantom of the Castle*.

JAMES D. JENKINS
CHICAGO, JUNE 6, 2005

WORKS BY RICHARD SICKELMORE

Novels[*]

Edgar; or, the Phantom of the Castle, 1798
Agnes and Leonora, 1799
Mary-Jane, 1800
Raymond, 1801
Rashleigh Abbey, or the Ruin on the Rock, 1805
Osrick, or Modern Horrors, 1809

Theatre

The Dream, a Serio-Dramatic Piece, 1797
Quarter Day, an Interlude, 1798
Saltimbanco; or, the Disagreeable Surprise, an Opera, 1798
The Cottage Maid; or, the Customs of the Castle, 1798
Aboukir Bay, or the Glorious First of August, 1799
Sketches from Life, a Comedy, 1802
A Birthday Tribute, an Interlude, 1805

ADDITIONAL READING ON SICKELMORE AND THE GOTHIC NOVEL

Frank, Frederick S. *The First Gothics*. New York: Garland
   Publishing, 1987.
Summers, Montague. *The Gothic Quest*. New York: Russell &
   Russell, 1964.

---

[*] Montague Summers also credits Sickelmore as the author of *The New Monk* (1798), a biting satire of Lewis's *The Monk*, published under the name "R.S.", but as it seems unlikely young Sickelmore would have published two such wildly different works as *Edgar* and *The New Monk* in the same year, and as Sickelmore's name always appears on the title pages of his other books, I have not included *The New Monk* in this list.

NOTE ON THE TEXT

The text of the Valancourt Books edition of *Edgar; or, the Phantom of the Castle* is based on the text of the only copy I was able to locate, the first edition housed in the Corvey Collection, a microfiche version of which is held by the University of Nebraska Libraries.

Edgar; or, the Phantom of the Castle was originally published at the Minerva Press for William Lane, London, 1798. It was translated into French as *Edgar; ou le Pouvoir du remords* and published Chez Moutradier, Paris, in 1800. Based on the bibliographical information available, I believe the present edition to be the second English-language edition of the novel, and the first reprinting in over two centuries.

In every possible instance, the original spellings, punctuation, and formatting have been retained. No attempt has been made to modernize or standardize spelling. Such apparent errors as "villany" for "villainy" and "falacious" for "fallacious" have been retained to capture the spirit of the original book. The name of one of the domestics is spelled, at various points in the novel, "Conrade," "Conrad," "Conard," and "Conrard"; I have changed all these to "Conrad" for consistency's sake. Two other obvious errors have also been corrected: a change from "summons" to "summon" in the phrase "ere I could summon sufficient courage" in Chapter XXVIII and "sooned" to "soon" in the sentence that begins, "They soon gained the ramparts of the fabric" in Chapter XXIX.

I would like to thank Kate Kane of the University of Nebraska Libraries' Microforms department for kindly providing me with the copy of the microfiche from which I typeset this new edition.

EDGAR;

OR, THE

PHANTOM OF THE CASTLE.

A NOVEL.

IN TWO VOLUMES.

BY

R. SICKELMORE.

" ———Foul deeds will rise,
" Though all the earth o'erwhelm them, to men's eyes."

VOL. I.

LONDON:
PRINTED AT THE
Minerva-Press,
FOR WILLIAM LANE, LEADENHALL-STREET.

M.DCC.XCVIII.

PREFACE.

BEFORE I permit the following pages to encounter the public eye, it is requisite I should make some apology for them. They were written with no other intention than to beguile my leisure hours of that torpidity which a disagreeable vacation of many months (ever incidental to the residents of watering-places) never failed to produce; more particularly so at Brighton, where the indefatigable exertions of three months must prove sufficiently lucrative to support the industrious mechanic for the remainder of the year. That I have endeavoured, by the only method in my power, to benefit my family, at a period, when I could have remained inactive, without reproach, I trust, will prove a motive too laudable for censure. Convinced that this simple tale is full of imperfections, should the keen glance of rigid criticism condescend to pass over it, I tremble for its fate;—yet, "conscious that I never wrote a line that would convey a wrong idea to the head, or a corrupt wish to the heart, I sit down perfectly satisfied with the purity of my intention,"—and embrace this opportunity of returning my acknowledgements to those friends who have encouraged and supported me in this publication, and sincerely hope they will not find any just cause, in its perusal, to reproach themselves with ill-timed liberality.

1

PREFACE

EDGAR;

OR, THE

PHANTOM OF THE CASTLE

CHAPTER I

————Strange things,
The neighbours say, have happen'd here;
Wild shrieks have issu'd from the hollow tombs:
Dead men have come again, and walk'd about:
And the great bell has toll'd, unrung, untouch'd.

BLAIR.

THE night was dark, the rain in torrents seemed to threaten the earth with a second deluge, "The lightning flash'd in vivid colours, and the thunder rolled in awful majesty,"

When Edgar, who almost exhausted, sought shelter from the storm within the mouldering walls of an old decayed priory.

The war of the agitated elements continued with renewed violence; and Edgar, who was not deficient in courage, determined to explore the more interior part of the desolated building, as the place where he then rested scarcely screened him from the rude attack of the hurricane.

He ascended a flight of steps, and with very little exertion forced open a door, which, cracking on its rusty hinges, admitted him into the building. Scarcely was he entered, when the

3

door closed with a ponderous crash, and defied the utmost strength of Edgar again to release it.

The tempest was now over the priory, the lightning flashed through the apertures of the dilapidated walls, while the loud thunder threatened the tottering ruin with instantaneous annihilation.

Edgar, impelled by fear for his own safety, as all retreat by the closing of the door was rendered ineffectual, descended a staircase, which he descried as the lightning illumined at intervals. He passed on as cautiously as the impenetrable darkness would admit, till his passage was obstructed by an iron door, which not being fastened, he with very little difficulty opened, and entered, to his infinite surprize, a large square room: a lamp hung suspended from the ceiling, which emitted a feeble glimmering light, hardly sufficient to pierce the extreme darkness which pervaded this gloomy apartment.

He stood for sometime to survey it. The faint light spread a tremulous gleam, more horrible than darkness itself.

Edgar was amazed at the incongruous appearance of this part of the structure, with the dilapidated walls he had just quitted; every thing here bore the aspect of having been lately occupied; and the lamp confirmed his suspicion beyond a doubt.

He retreated a few paces, undetermined whether he should proceed any further, or trace his way back, which he could easily effect, with the assistance of the light. This he immediately seized; at the same instant recollecting, that should he reach the place by which he entered, unheard, he had no way of escaping, as the closing of the door had rendered it impracticable:—a circumstance he till that moment had totally forgot.

For the first time, he felt himself appalled by fear. It might be the residence of a banditti; but as certainty is less painful than suspense, he determined to push forward and boldly meet his fate.

This room conducted him to a winding passage of considerable extent, and was at length closed by a door, which Edgar, though with extreme labour, burst open, it being fastened on the inside; when the wind gushing from the aperture, extinguished the light.

Edgar was now in a truly deplorable situation. To grope his way back, had he been ever so inclined, was impossible; and to proceed forward, equally, if not more hazardous.

He was alarmed by a violent and uncommon noise, which seemed to resound from the extremity of the place he had just forced open. Now, thought Edgar, the crisis of my adventure is approaching, and stood absorbed in silent terror.

The stillness had for some time remained undisturbed; Edgar, ashamed of his fear, entered the apartment, and was agreeably surprized by the appearance of a ray of light, which streamed through a crevice of a door, exactly opposite to where he then stood.

The fear of robbers was at this critical juncture entirely forgot. But ere he had reached that part of the fabric from whence he descried the glimmering, it rushed with renovated energy into his mind, and with it, all its attendant horrors.

He hesitated, unresolved; hope and fear alternately supported or depressed his spirits. He at last summoned up sufficient resolution to call out, accompanying his voice with a loud rap at the door.

The trembling gleam which had at first renewed his courage, vanished; and all was again concealed in silent darkness.

Edgar now redoubled his shouts; which echoing through the gloomy avenues of the edifice, increased the terrors of his situation.

He now endeavoured to force the door, but in this he was not so successful as he had hitherto been; and though despair had given him treble strength and resolution, it defied his most intense efforts even to make it tremble in its frame.

The sound of footsteps was now distinctly heard; Edgar listened attentively; they seemed approaching toward him; he trembled, and remained fixed in anxious expectation—some one ran against him. Edgar stretched out his arm and endeavoured to seize him; but the person eluded his grasp, and retreated with the greatest precipitancy.

Edgar being a little recovered from his surprize, endeavoured to trace the way by which he entered, as every means of proceeding forward was entirely cut off; when his hand, accidentally, in groping his passage, struck against a key, which projected from a lock; this he with avidity turned, shoved back a door, and found himself at the foot of a staircase, which he in haste began to ascend; when instantly a noise, as of many footsteps, re-echoed from below, and a sudden burst of light discovered to him a kind of recess, a little to the right, which he with more precipitation than prudence, entered: the floor gave way, and he fell with violence through the aperture.

Edgar, quite stunned by the fall, remained for some time insensible; and a considerable space of time had elapsed, after he recovered, before he could summon to his memory the casualty which had thus deprived him of his reason.

The apartment, or rather dungeon, where he then reclined, being on the ground-floor, the chill damps and vapours which curled round him, together with the horrid stench which he inhaled, had nearly again robbed him of his faculties.

It was plain he had fallen through the floor above; but as no fragments of the shattered boards had fallen with him, he conceived it must have been a trap-door through which he had so disagreeably descended.

A faint breeze, which seemed to force its entrance from the opposite extremity of this dreary cell, with a radiant stream of day-light, quickly revived him.

He arose, and hastened with anxious steps (as he imagined) to the grate, that he might more purely enjoy the fresh morning air.

His foot struck against something, he stumbled, and had nearly fallen; he stooped to examine what it was, and his hand rested on the face of a human being, cold, putrid, and clammy!

His blood recoiled with horror; big drops of sweat hung trembling on his brow, and he involuntarily stepped back. During a pause of some moments he regained his equanimity, and quickened his pace till he reached the other part of this solitary abode. What ecstasy filled his mind, when he discovered, that what he at first conceived to be only a grating, proved a large aperture in the wall; occasioned, as he rightly conjectured, by a part of the decayed building falling in the late tempest, and, alighting on this part of the fabric, had pierced it almost to the foundation!

Though the gap was several feet above the level of the ground where Edgar stood, and even with the surface of the earth without, he found very little difficulty in effecting his emancipation, as an immense quantity of the rubbish had fallen inward, and rendered it an easy ascent.

Never did Edgar experience a sensation of greater delight than that moment produced which freed him from his loathsome prison. His joy, however, was transitory; a retrospect of unpleasant events, and what possibly might next occur, to harrass and depress him; in his present unprotected state, curbed the farther progression of his bliss, and raised the baneful traits of sorrow on his manly countenance.

He took one last cursory view of the edifice, and walked silent and disconsolate away.

CHAPTER II

Why, let the stricken deer go weep,
 The heart ungall'd go play;
For some must watch, while some must sleep:
 Thus runs the world away.

SHAKESPEARE.

THE rosy blush of day now sparkled in the east; not a vestige remained of the devastations of the night, except the shattered fragments of the priory, scattered about the forest by the resistless fury of the storm. The delighted choristers on the spray began to chirp their melodious matins, all Nature smiled, and seemed to hail the rising majesty of Day.

Edgar proceeded forward until he had reached Bardolph's cottage on the skirts of the forest. This, said he, will sanctuarise me from present pursuit, and its occupier will welcome me with the rapture of unfeigned friendship.

Bardolph had been the faithful follower of his deceased father, and to Edgar he had ever been firmly attached; though his artless and benevolent disposition might have gained him the good-will of those less frequently with him than was Bardolph.

Edgar's form was strikingly handsome, nor was his mind less accomplished: he had early imbibed almost every requisite that distinguishes the gentleman. Brought up under the eye of one of the best of fathers, who paid him every attention, suffered no expence to be spared that might contribute to render his darling boy an ornament and a blessing to society: and liberally was he repaid for his labour, in contemplating the dawning virtues of his son, which early promised to make him the counterpart of himself.

Edgar had no sooner entered Bardolph's humble tenement, than the honest veteran, with heartfelt joy rose up to receive

8

him; expressing at the same time his surprize and apprehension at the haggard appearance of Edgar's countenance. I hope, continued Bardolph, the Baron, your uncle, and all friends at the castle are well?—All, replied Edgar, when I left them; but pray, good Bardolph, cease all interrogatories for the present, and conduct me to some place where I may rest my aching limbs, for I have been excessively harrassed and fatigued; by-and-by you shall find me willing to satisfy you every enquiry.

Bardolph, without replying, conducted him to his own apartment. This, your Honour, said he, as he opened the door of the chamber, is the best room my humble dwelling affords; but such as it is, you are heartily welcome to. Edgar expressed his satisfaction, and Bardolph retired. Being left by himself, he endeavoured to find a transitory suspension from his sorrow in the arms of Morpheus.

I am afraid, said Bardolph, as he reseated himself by the fire, all does not go well at castle Fitz-Elmar.

I am apprehensive so, likewise, answered Dorothy; but no matter, for, exclusive of Master Edgar and Miss Helen, nobody cares a brass farthing about them.

It strikes me, exclaimed Bardolph, that Master Edgar has quitted the castle unknown to his uncle.

Well, replied Dorothy, and had I been Master Edgar, I had done as much long ere this, if I had been as cruelly treated by that unfeeling brute the Baron:—A wonderful and grievous change has poor Edgar experienced since his dear father was inhumanly murdered in the forest.

Prithee be silent, Dorothy, replied Bardolph, we shall disturb our guest; and besides you know I do not like to have that subject mentioned.

No more does the Baron, answered Dorothy, with a significant toss of her head.

The Baron (vociferated Bardolph, with extreme vehemence) is a ——

What is he? cried Dorothy.

No matter, growled out Bardolph, curbing his rising choler, women should not be trusted too far; however, time I hope will discover everything, and then, *woe be to the guilty.*

Whom do you allude to? said Dorothy eagerly; and what am I to understand by—woe be to the guilty?

Bardolph having entered a little further into the subject than he at first intended, he dared not trust himself with another reply, but hastily, to the great disappointment of Dorothy, withdrew; who now anxiously waited the time of Edgar's rising, that she might learn from himself the cause of his appearing at so early an hour at her cottage, and so many miles distant from castle Fitz-Elmar.

CHAPTER III

—— O treacherous Night,
Thou lendest thy ready veil to every treason;
And teeming mischiefs thrive beneath thy shade.

HILL.

EDGAR, as if on purpose to weary the patience of Dorothy, continued fast locked in the downy arms of Morpheus, and did not again make his appearance till bright Sol had finished his diurnal round, and twilight's sable mantle had enveloped half the world, as if in mourning for the god's departure.

Bardolph returned some hours previous to Edgar's rising; and no sooner heard him descending the stairs than he rose up with alacrity once more to give him a hearty welcome to his cottage.

Dorothy, placing him a chair, requested him to seat himself, loading her table, at the same time, with such provisions as her humble dwelling afforded, imagining his appetite at this period must be very urgent, as he had not broken his fast during the whole of the day.

Bardolph, said Edgar, after he had finished his frugal repast, you was with my father when he met with that melancholy catastrophe in the forest?

Aye, replied Bardolph, and ever will it be engraven in legible characters on my heart.

If you remember it, Bardolph, replied Edgar, well may his persecuted unprotected son. — The big round tear stood trembling in his eye as he spoke.

Dorothy was moved, and Bardolph drew out his pocket-handkerchief to blow his nose.

11

I wish you to inform me, good Bardolph, continued Edgar, the particulars of that unfortunate event, as I have never heard it but imperfectly stated.

It is now above three years since, as your Honour may remember, that the late Sir Edgar, and myself his faithful Esquire, was returning from the holy wars, we were benighted on this dreary forest, about seven short miles distant from castle Fitz-Elmar, when the lowring sky, the hollow murmuring of the rising wind, and every other symptom that portends a tempest, induced us to clap spurs to our horses, and hasten on with more than usual alacrity. We had scarcely proceeded half a mile when the storm assailed us with such rapid violence, that we were necessitated, for our better security, to endeavour to discover some place where we might shelter ourselves until the tremendous fury of the hurricane became a little subsided. An old ruin, which stands nearly in the centre of the forest, met our sight; we immediately turned our horses, and were advancing toward it, when we were suddenly attacked by a ruthless gang of banditti. Sir Edgar drew his sword, and put himself into a posture of defence; I followed his example, determined to sell our lives as dear as possible, for murder seemed to be their sole intent. For a considerable time we sustained the unequal contest, until Sir Edgar, covered with wounds, fell senseless from his horse; some of the banditti immediately dismounted, and with repeated stabs terminated the life of one of the best of men and of masters.

Edgar, no longer able to contain his emotion, sobbed aloud; and old Dorothy sat petrified with horror, for she had never heard Bardolph say so much on the subject before. A short time elapsed ere Edgar regained his composure, when Bardolph resumed his melancholy narration.

His murder was certainly premeditated, your Honour, for each time those damned villains raised their accursed weapons to pierce the breast of the renowned Sir Edgar, I heard these words audibly pronounced: — This for our fallen comrades (three of whom were slain in this bloody combat, who with horrid execrations bit the dust, and expired in the greatest agonies) and this for the reward.

O thou omnipotent Disposer of all things (exclaimed Edgar, dropping on his knees) grant me but this, my most fervent obsecration, that I may discover the assassins who perpetrated the horrid deed, become the instrument of thy divine vengeance to punish this diabolical act of villany, and I have nothing more to ask!

Edgar, drying up the tears of sad remembrance, which had collected in his eyes, and were trickling down his face in mournful succession, requested Bardolph to go on with his narrative.

Perceiving, continued Bardolph, that I could render no farther assistance to my dear Master, and the only chance of my escaping was by flight, I suddenly turned my horse's head, struck the spurs into his hide (and being well mounted) he darted forward, and soon left the ruffians, though several pursued me, a considerable distance behind. Your Honour knows the rest. I was some months before I recovered of my wounds; and Sir Edgar, with the three robbers, was found the subsequent morning, quite dead, in the forest.

I vow and protest, quoth Dorothy, if I had imagined your relation would have *horrified* a body in such a manner, I would not have sat to have heard the conclusion of it. I declare I sha'nt be myself again these two hours.

Edgar was lost in reverie; but being interrogated by Bardolph respecting the procedure at the castle, it roused him from his stupor; and having a little collected his spirits, he proceeded to satisfy Bardolph's urgent solicitation.

During the first year after the demise of my father, the Baron treated me with extreme tenderness; and his truly paternal behaviour reconciled me, in a manner, to the loss of my parent; but never could make me forget him, for that were impossible. But the Baron had sinister views in thus endeavouring to make my situation pleasant to me: I was to espouse his daughter, or no longer be considered as his nephew. Wherefore, no sooner was he given to understand it was not in my power to acquiesce with what he had planned for my future establishment, than this arch fiend (for he merits no better appellation) dropped the mask; and conceived that what I had refused to comply with by gentle treatment, might be effected, by proving to me how much I was in his power: and with the iron hand of despotic authority, made me acutely feel the loss I had sustained in the best of fathers. Twelve months have I endured the repeated insults of this inhuman tyrant. One year more, and my majority would place me above his power; and until the arrival of that period, I will no more enter the walls of Castle Fitz-Elmar: wherefore, you see me now a poor forlorn wanderer, without friends, and without a home; but with that true spirit of independence which will ever make me spurn at tyranny and oppression, let it appear in whatsoever shape it may.

Edgar then recited to them his adventure in the forest; and expressed (at some future period) his determination to revisit the old ruin, and urgently requested that Bardolph would accompany him.

Bardolph was evidently too much astonished to return an immediate answer; and old Dorothy, who did not hesitate to pronounce the adventure at the priory, to be occasioned by ghosts and hobgoblins, quite overcome by fear, drew her chair nearer to the fire, and trembled with apprehension, lest Bardolph should give an assent to Edgar's proposal.

However, Bardolph's reply was prevented by a loud knocking at the door. Dorothy uttered a scream, and flew to Edgar for protection; imagining nothing less than a troop of spectres would be thus clamorous in disturbing the tranquillity of her humble dwelling. Bardolph, springing from his seat to the door, enquired, without opening it, who and what they were? and what their business was with him? was answered in a hoarse discordant tone (which Bardolph immediately knew to be Bernardine's, one of the Baron's menials) that his young master, Edgar Fitz-Elmar, had absconded from his uncle, and no person at the castle knew what was become of him; and that the Baron had dispatched him and several more of the domestics, different roads, in search of the runaway; particularly cautioning me not to neglect calling at your cottage; and to command you, at your peril, to refuse giving me such information as might be within your knowledge; as he does not hesitate to pronounce you to be in colleague with his nephew. Bardolph, still keeping the door closed, replied he knew nothing of the affair, and that he was excessively grieved and surprised at his unpleasant intelligence; and more so that the Baron should suspect him of assisting Edgar in withdrawing from the castle; but that he would wait on the Baron the subsequent morning, when he did not doubt but he should be able to evince him how fallacious his suspicions were.

The fellow pretended to be satisfied with this answer, and walked off: and Edgar (after about an hour's conversation with Bardolph on what means to adopt to elude the vigilance of the Baron and his emissaries, but without determining on any thing) separated for the night; purposing to put in practice, early in the morning, whatever scheme could possibly be devised that might effectually secure him from the future machinations of his tyrannic uncle.

CHAPTER IV

Now turn your eyes to yon sweet-smelling bow'r,
Where, flush'd with all the insolence of wealth,
Sits pamper'd Vice! For him th'Arabian gale
Breathes forth delicious odours; Gallia's hills
For him pour nectar from the purple vine.
Nor think for these he pays the tribute due
To Heav'n: of Heav'n he never names the name,
Save when with imprecations dark and dire
He points his jest obscene.

Dr. Glynn.

If he were open'd, and you find so much blood
in his liver as would clog the foot of a flea, I'll eat
the rest of the anatomy.

Shakespeare.

IT may not be unpleasant to the reader, before we proceed any further with our history, to be made acquainted with past events.

The present Baron Fitz-Elmar, and our hero's father, Sir Edgar Fitz-Elmar, were own brothers; but as different in principles and disposition as the extremes of good and bad could possibly be delineated.

The Baron was overbearing, morose, proud, ambitious; never forgiving the person who had but for once offended him; trampling the laws of God and man beneath his feet, if found necessary to obtain his wishes; was vindictive, sanguinary, but withal the arrantest coward that ever disgraced manhood.

Being the elder brother, the title of Baron devolved to him on the demise of his father, together with castle Fitz-Elmar, and other estates of immense value.

Soon after the decease of his father, he espoused a lady of noble lineage; which was, in fact, his principal motive in marrying her (though avaricious in the extreme): hereditary

16

honours he conceived almost equivalent for every fault, but small fortune. Had he been of a less turbulent disposition, they might have lived happy together; for his lady, though not one of the evenest of tempers, was rather inclined to the placable than the clamorous: however, a diurnal round of his brutal behaviour, in a few months after their marriage, entirely soured what portion of moderation she possessed, that their hours glided away in one continued course of discord and confusion. About five years after their union, he contrived to finish part of their noisy career, by hurrying her out of the world.

One daughter, the only offspring of this connexion, he at that period appeared to be excessively fond of; which, as she advanced to years of maturity, he instilled into her tender mind those principles most congenial with his own: nor was her person more perfect than her mind; for, to use the words of an eminent and admired author,—

> "Her face most filthy was to see,
> With squinting eyes, contrary ways extended,
> And loathly mouth unfit a mouth to be,
> Which nought but gall and venom comprehended,
> And wicked words that God and man offended."

Sir Edgar Fitz-Elmar—— But the least compliment we can pay to so distinguished a personage, will be to give him a chapter to himself.

CHAPTER V

His life was gentle; and the elements
So mixt in him, that Nature might stand up,
And say to all the world, This was a man.

SHAKESPEARE.

SIR Edgar Fitz-Elmar, though a younger brother, the fortune he inherited from his father was by no means contemptible, for, independent of the considerable landed property which devolved to the elder brother, the late Baron died worth some considerable sums of money; the whole of which he bequeathed to his younger son, who two years preceding his father's death, had married an amiable lady of good family and large fortune, that his circumstances were equal, if not superior, to his brother's.

Sir Edgar was liberal, noble, and just, possessed of undaunted courage and resolution sufficient to brave all peril. He conceived that enterprises the most bold and hazardous, by perseverance, could be overcome. In the field of battle he appeared with that cool determined valour which ever marks the experienced and hardy veteran.

"An eye like Mars, to threaten or command:
Though terrible in battle, he
Could shew by godlike clemency,
He grac'd the wreath he won."

The distinguished title of Knight-Banneret he had gained in his first crusade against the infidels, while his brother was revelling in all the insolence of pride and hereditary honours at home.

Castle Fitz-Elmar, being once the favourite residence of his father, became in consequence the favourite retirement of Sir

18

Edgar; and a few months after the old Baron was interred, he purchased it at an exorbitant price of his avaricious brother. Thither he retired with his family, where he continued for some years, blessed in all the endearments of conjugal affection and domestic felicity. His benevolence was unbounded.

He wiped away the briny tears of tribulation from the pallid cheek of poverty. In him the wretched ever found a friend. Thus lived Sir Edgar; doing good to all around him; loving and beloved by all mankind.

CHAPTER VI

Misfortune does not always wait on Vice;
Nor is Success the constant guest of Virtue.—
Perhaps the Gods more amiably design
To shew the hero, struggling in the toils
Of unforeseen, unmerited distress.—
The great example beams instruction forth;
And better serves the purposes of Heav'n.

HAVARD.

YOUNG Edgar was about fifteen years of age, when the general happiness which prevailed at the castle, was suddenly terminated by the death of that pattern of female excellence Lady Fitz-Elmar.

For some time after this irremediable misfortune, Sir Edgar remained inconsolable. He would shut himself up in his room and not even suffer young Edgar, of whom he was passionately fond, to intrude upon his melancholy retirement. Several months elapsed in this distressing state of apathy, till time, the soother of the acutest anguish, in a small degree, reconciled him to his destiny.

"Hope left the heart, yet patience met the rod,
And prov'd the man a particle of God."

About this time he received intelligence of his sovereign's undertaking another crusade against the infidels, and that numbers of cavaliers, anxious to signalize themselves in the field of arms, had flocked to his standard.

No sooner was Sir Edgar acquainted with the king's intention than he determined to accompany him; once more to dedicate his service to his prince, humble the unbelievers of the christian religion, and try, if possible, to forget his own calamity amidst the noise and din of war.

Sir Edgar having formed this resolution, immediately wrote to his brother, the Baron, who was at this period in the metropolis, requesting his immediate presence at castle Fitz-Elmar. On his arrival he informed him of his determination; and, in case this last expedition should terminate his life, he designed to leave him sole executor, and guardian to his son, that every thing should continue under his jurisdiction during Edgar's minority; at the expiration of which time he should deliver up every thing to his nephew, after deducting three thousand marks for his maintenance, and other articles he might hereafter have occasion for. And should his son not survive his minority, castle Fitz-Elmar, together with the whole of what he possessed, should devolve to the Baron's daughter.

This charge his brother, seemingly, with great reluctance accepted; and proper writings, expressive of the above, were immediately made out, sealed, and signed.

Sir Edgar, thus made happy respecting the future protection of his son, recovered a small portion of his long abdicated vivacity; for where could his boy, the child of his beloved Emma, be so safe as with his uncle? Possessing no guile himself, he never suspected it in others, or his cooler judgment must have informed him that his brother was the most improper man in existence to be selected as guardian to his son.

The hour of parting arrived; Sir Edgar was unusually sad; a something whispered him, as he clasped his darling boy to his heart, that this would be the last time they should ever meet. He embraced his brother, and, as the briny drops were trickling down his face, requested he would pay every attention to his child. He gave the hand of his son into that of his brother.— My dear Armine, faintly articulated Sir Edgar, sobs almost choking his utterance, prove a kind, a tender protector to my boy, my dear, my only child, the child of my sainted Emma; so may God prosper thee and thine—long mayest thou rule, undisturbed, amidst the endearing smiles of thine own happy family, and never experience the fell stings of unmerited disappointment which now rends the breast of thy unhappy brother.—But hold, impious, let me not censure the decree of the Almighty! when God wills it shall be so, frail man should be resigned.

Sir Armine, with every protestation best suited to deceive Sir Edgar, received the hand of his nephew from his brother, who bidding an affectionate farewell to the rest of the family, once more embraced his boy, and hurried off to join the standard of his sovereign.

CHAPTER VII

What havock hast thou made, foul monster, Sin,
Greatest and first of ills! the fruitful parent
Of woes of all dimensions! but for thee,
Sorrow had never been.

BLAIR.

NEAR two years had elapsed since the departure of Sir Edgar, without any thing worthy of moment occurring, except the officiousness of Lucretia, the Baron's daughter, in endeavouring to make herself agreeable in the eyes of our hero; but without effect. Edgar ever addressed her with that attentive politeness due to the daughter of his father's brother; but her half-suppressed sighs, and the tender glances of her bright oblique orbs, he treated with that frigid indifference which an impartial observer would rather have imputed to antipathy, than the dawning of that passion which the divine Lucretia would sometimes flatter herself she had inspired him with.

Sir Armine understood the human physiognomy too well to be deceived in this respect, and oftentimes marked Edgar's behaviour to his daughter with every trait of disappointment and disapprobation depicted on his own features.

He is young and thoughtless, exclaimed the Baron, one day to his daughter, as Edgar quitted the room, after having defied the gorgon eyes of his angelic cousin, the tender scrutiny of which he had borne with more than the usual apparent portion of disgust, to make any impression on his obduracy, or want of taste—He is young and thoughtless, my child; time no doubt will make him sensible, if not to his own interest, to the charms of my dear Lucretia.

Provoking, insufferable monster, blubbered Lucretia, almost bursting with passion, and traversing the apartment in all the majesty of an enraged vixen; though he were my aversion—

were he as hateful to my sight as a venomous toad, I would marry him, that I might have it in my power to punish him for this diabolical, insupportable, haughty indifference.

Be composed, my dear Lucretia, replied Sir Armine; time, as I observed before, I have no doubt will make him all we wish. This I will assure my sweet girl, continued the Baron, grinding his teeth, castle Fitz-Elmar shall never boast a mistress, save my dear Lucretia.

The reader, no doubt, is acquainted ere this, that the noble Baron had determined within himself, from the moment of Sir Edgar's departure, that his daughter should possess his brother's immense wealth by a marriage with young Edgar, trusting he should have our hero so much in dread of his power, that the deformity of Lucretia's person would not be a sufficient inducement in the breast of the nephew, to thwart the wishes of the uncle.

He, however, imagined that if this grand point could be effected by gentle measures, it would be the more agreeable to all parties, and he himself should escape the calumny of a censorious world: but should Edgar, as he advanced to years of maturity, be averse to join his hand in the Hymeneal chain with Lucretia, to adopt such means to enforce him to compliance as he might hereafter devise. He imparted his design to Lucretia, who readily acquiesced in every thing he proposed. In consequence of which lenient resolve, our hero was suffered to follow the bent of his own inclination to this period, when their future machinations were likely to be rendered abortive by a letter from Sir Edgar, whom they had already began to conceive was no more, it being now nearly on the verge of eighteen months since they had received any account of him; and many noblemen, embarked in the same cause with himself, in the course of that time had fallen in the sanguifluous bed of honour, of whom no particular accounts had ever been transmitted.

The letter from Sir Edgar announced him already on his passage to England, and that a few weeks, at farthest, would safely conduct him to castle Fitz-Elmar; and requested the Baron, his family, and his dear boy would be there to receive him.

The Baron, on perusing the letter, was evidently embarrassed; but forcing his dark unblushing features into a smile, he turned to Edgar and Lucretia, who at this time were both present, and acquainted them with the contents of Sir Edgar's epistle. Lucretia had kept her eyes steadily fixed on her father, and, in the lineaments of his countenance read the counterpart of her own. As for Edgar (too much enraptured by this joyful intelligence particularly to notice any thing) he laughed, cried, sung, danced, and committed a thousand extravagancies, which expressed his extreme joy and dutiful affection.

However, Sir Armine, apparently agreeable to his brother's request, set off the next day, with all his family, for castle Fitz-Elmar, having first dispatched a messenger to Conrad, an old faithful domestic of Sir Edgar's, with whom the castle had been left in charge, to have every thing ready for his reception.

CHAPTER VIII

The drowsy night grows on the world, and now
The busy craftsman and o'erlabour'd hind
Forget the travail of the day in sleep.
* * * * * * * * * * * * * *
What noise is that?
What visitor is this, who with bold freedom
Breaks in upon the peaceful night and rest,
With such a rude approach?

ROWE.

ABOUT three weeks after the arrival of Sir Armine at the castle, he received a second letter from his brother, announcing his return to England, and that the day subsequent to the morrow, he would join his dear brother at castle Fitz-Elmar.

The whole of this day the Baron was closetted with Bernardine; who, as we shall have occasion frequently to mention in the course of this history, it may not be unpleasant to the reader to be made acquainted with his person and principles.

Bernardine's figure would almost have terrified an honest man to gaze at: a large scar crossed his forehead, which terminating a little below the left eye, or rather a little below the socket of the eye, for the unfortunate casualty which had indented his forehead, had likewise deprived him of that useful luminary; his nose was large and curved, and graced with a prodigious quantity of flaming carbuncles; his mouth was twisted nearly under the right ear, and had once been ornamented with a charming set of black and yellow grinders, which by some accident or other, were now almost broken from the jaw: in addition to which—a black bushy beard, scowling brows, and a profusion of dirty, greasy, matted hair, rendered him as complete a monster of ugliness as the most consummate scoundrel would wish to employ to perpetrate an

26

act of villany: nor was his heart less deformed than his face. He was, nevertheless, the favourite of Sir Armine, and was recently employed by him as watchman; though it was very well understood by the domestics collectively, that he seldom was within the Baron's premises after sun-set.

This man then, on the whole of that day on which arrived Sir Edgar's second letter, was the Baron in close conference with, as he had likewise been several days previously, but without being once remarked by Edgar; for his spirits were so much exhilarated with the expectation of soon embracing his parent, that he had no time to notice, or in fact, to think of any thing else.

One incident, however, must not be omitted, which occurred the night preceding the day on which Sir Edgar was expected. Our hero had retired to his chamber, though somewhat later than customary, and finding it impossible to sleep (for the idea of the morrow had banished his repose) he endeavoured to amuse himself by reading, when he was interrupted by the sound of voices under his window. He arose gently, and with as little noise as possible opened the casement; but the night being intensely dark and tempestuous, hid the interlocutors from his sight. He thought he could distinguish Bernardine's voice; and the other, though spoken in a lower key, he imagined was not unlike the Baron's; however, this was merely conjecture, the rising wind preventing his hearing much of their discourse; nor indeed did he wish it, and was going to close the window, when his own name and that of his father's he heard audibly pronounced. Edgar now listened more attentively; but could make nothing out of what passed, until just as they were about to separate—when the person, whose voice he had conceived not unlike his uncle's, replied, — Bring me sure tidings of his death, and expect the promised reward. They then parted; and Edgar, seized with an unusual tremor, flung too the sash. He dreaded he knew not what; and in a state

27

quite the reverse from that he entered the apartment, threw himself upon the bed, accompanied with every sensation the foregoing scene had excited, anxiously waiting the return of day.

He had lain in this state above two hours, when he was again alarmed by a violent knocking at the castle-portal; and in a short time after, the whole edifice rang with the cries of Bardolph. Edgar immediately knew his voice, and rushed down stairs into the hall, where Bardolph had been admitted by one of the domestics whom the noise at the portal had roused.

Bardolph, severely wounded, and almost fainting with loss of blood, had yet strength sufficient to inform Edgar of the catastrophe in the forest, before recited, ere he fainted in the arms of the servant who supported him. Edgar was speechless, "horror struck upon his heart," and he dropped senseless at the feet of the expiring Bardolph.

CHAPTER IX

Life's but a walking shadow; a poor player,
That struts and frets his hour upon the stage,
And then is heard no more.
                                        SHAKESPEARE.

THE servant, extremely alarmed at the situation of Edgar and
Bardolph, soon disturbed the rest of the household; even the
noble Baron himself condescended personally, and half un-
dressed, to descend into the hall, and demanded the cause of
this sudden and unusual tumult? The domestic interrogated
made no reply, but with his finger, pointed to Edgar, and the
apparently expiring Bardolph.

"His silver skin lac'd with his golden blood,
And his gash'd stabs, look'd like a breach in nature,
For ruin's wasteful entrance."

The Baron started back, his lips quivered, and for some
moments he was deprived of the power of speech.

Sir Edgar Fitz-Elmar is dead, murdered in the forest by a
banditti; and honest Bardolph, his faithful attendant, is dying,
exclaimed the man who had heard the recital of Bardolph to
Edgar. And master Edgar, replied another, appears defunct
likewise.

The Baron shortly regained his composure, and with
trembling accents, which rather denoted some secret apprehension that more had been discovered than would redound to the
credit of his own sweet person, or commiseration for the poor
sufferers, articulated, My brother and Bardolph both dead! and
my poor Edgar in a state hardly less alarming! Oh! Heaven,
this is too, too much for—— Here he broke off abruptly, and
introducing some well-feigned heart-breaking sobs, which fully

29

answered the purpose he designed them, by steeping the whole group of sorrowful faces in tears, which so completely blinded their perception, that his own hypocritical countenance was effectually hid from too minute an observation, which he had at first imagined was bestowed upon him by the domestics in general:—so ready is guilt to construe every occurrence to its own disadvantage.

A loud groan from Bardolph curdled the Baron's blood, who with tremulous voice ejaculated, Heaven and earth! Bardolph not dead! — immediately recollecting himself, but being too much overpowered by his own feelings to utter another word, or fearing he had said too much already, he threw himself into a chair, and was, for some time, in a situation very little superior to Edgar's.

Miss Lucretia, who had been listening at the door, now rushed into the hall, and clamorously bewailed the dire misfortune which had thus deprived her of her dearly beloved and ever-to-be-lamented uncle.

The Baron now, though his words were scarcely audible, ordered Bardolph and Edgar to be conveyed to bed, and a surgeon immediately sent for; then, with the assistance of his daughter, left the hall and tottered toward his own apartment.

After the surgeon had visited his patients, the Baron had given orders that he might be conducted into his chamber; which being done, he with much anxiety and perturbation, interrogated the surgeon respecting the wounded Bardolph: and as the surgeon expressed his apprehension that the wounds of Bardolph, particularly two across his left temple, were mortal, a smile of joy illumined Sir Armine's features; but, as if afraid to continue there, immediately vanished, and was succeeded by an appearance of extreme dejection, apparently occasioned by the dubious account he had just heard of the honest veteran.

The surgeon was called away from the Baron to attend on poor Edgar; who only recovered from one swoon to relapse into another, till nature seemed quite exhausted, and left him so enfeebled, that for several weeks he had not strength sufficient to quit his apartment; during which time Bardolph had been pronounced out of danger, and, at his own request, removed to his cottage on the skirts of the forest, which had been assigned to him by his late master Sir Edgar, and was occupied by old Dorothy his wife, who had only left it since the catastrophe in the forest, to nurse her wounded husband at the castle.

Sir Edgar had been interred with great funeral pomp, and Castle Fitz-Elmar once more wore the external appearance of tranquillity.

CHAPTER X

They lov'd; but such their guileless passion was,
As in the dawn of time inform'd the heart
Of innocence and undissembling truth.

THOMSON.

OUR hero recovered but slowly: for several months he continued in a melancholy state of convalescence before he entirely
regained his health; nor could the assiduous attention of Sir
Armine, who redoubled his endearments to him, dispel the
gloom which had entirely deprived him of his wonted portion
of vivacity.

An occurrence, at this epocha took place, which again
animated the dormant faculties of Edgar, and once more
rendered the castle, which had of late become the object of his
silent antipathy, the boundary of all his wishes; and could he
have followed the path prescribed by his own virtuous inclination, not an idea, at this period, would have strayed beyond it.

Sir Armine had received information of the death of Sir
Marmaduke Cauvand, a worthy gentleman to whom he was
under infinite obligations (which, not directly interfering with
this history, would be tedious to enumerate) and one for whom
he had often warmly professed the most unalterable friendship:
That Sir Marmaduke had bequeathed to his care an only
daughter, until the arrival of her brother in England, who was
at this period in Italy, but to whom letters had been dispatched
prior to Sir Marmaduke's death, acquainting him of the precarious state of his father's health, and requesting his presence, in
all good speed, so that his return might in a short space of time
be expected.

This epistle likewise informed the Baron, that Sir Marmaduke had left twelve thousand marks, the whole of his
fortune, jointly between his son and daughter. Inclosed was

likewise a few lines, written by Sir Marmaduke himself, but a few hours previous to his dissolution, conjuring Sir Armine, by every term that affection for his children or friendship to the Baron could dictate, to proffer the lenient, protecting hand of a parent to his dear Helen, and admit her a welcome inmate at castle Fitz-Elmar, until the return of his dear boy.

Sir Armine, thus invoked, immediately set off for the metropolis, perfectly convinced that the trouble he should experience would be the only inconvenience he should suffer, in consequence of his complying with his friend's request; as the lady was in possession of more than sufficient to defray every expence he might incur on her account. Had Sir Marmaduke died poor, and Sir Armine been applied to for pecuniary assistance for his children, it is most probable he would not so readily have acquiesced.

Sir Armine, in due time arrived in London, performed every requisite, and returned with the blooming Helen to castle Fitz-Elmar.

> "Her form was fresher than the morning rose
> When the dew wets its leaves; unstain'd, and pure
> As is the lily, or the mountain-snow."

Our hero was astonished at the beauty and elegance of her person: he had never witnessed so much loveliness before—an ineffable sensation thrilled upon his heart as he stood absorbed in admiration and surprise; while the beauteous Helen,

> "Unconscious of her pow'r, and turning quick
> With unaffected blushes from his gaze,
> He saw her charming, but he saw not half
> The charms her downcast modesty conceal'd.
> That very moment love and chaste desire
> Sprung in his bosom."

Scarcely had a few weeks elapsed ere Helen silently acknowledged the superior merit of Edgar; while the Baron, with every mark of displeasure, watched, with lynx's eye, their growing passion.

Six months had expired since Helen had been residentiary at the castle, and no letters had been received from her brother. The Baron began to grow impatient; the presence of Helen became irksome to him; and Lucretia was possessed of too much penetration not to perceive that Helen was tenderly beloved by Edgar, and that Edgar, in return, was no less admired by Helen.

The result of which discovery was, that Edgar was summoned to attend his uncle in the library; and the plan which the noble Baron had formed in his own mind, for his future establishment, there made known to him. This Edgar, though diffidently, peremptorily refused to comply with; which so exasperated his uncle, that had not our hero made his escape by flight from his presence, we know not how far the Baron's rage might have hurried him.

Nearly twelve months from this interview did Edgar silently endure the diurnal insults and reproaches from his inhuman uncle; nor was Helen, to whom no account had yet been transmitted from her brother, less subject to the clamorous rebukes of Lucretia.

Edgar at last determined to abandon the castle; he privately conveyed a note to Helen, informing her of his intention until the expiration of his minority, when he would return to take possession of castle Fitz-Elmar, and claim the hand of his dear Helen as a reward for his unalterable love and fidelity.

This resolution once formed, Edgar found very little difficulty in putting it into execution.

The day preceding the night on which Edgar effected his emancipation, in crossing the hall he encountered Bernardine. The sounds he had distinctly heard under his window the night of his father's death, recurred to his memory, and though, for

34

prudential reasons, he had never mentioned to any one, he now determined to demand an explanation of Bernardine; for which purpose he thus accosted him: — "Bernardine, with whom was you discoursing, near the east wing of the castle, the evening on which my father lost his life in the forest? Surely your business must be very extraordinary to induce you to encounter the inclemency of the elements on such a tempestuous night, when you might have been more pleasantly accommodated in the castle!"

Bernardine trembled; his rotten stumps chattered in his head as he hurried from Edgar, without even deigning a reply; so consummately did he appear embarrassed and confounded.

Edgar, now confirmed in his suspicions, exclaimed—a time will come when the secrets of that evening shall be wrung from thy facinorous heart.

No sooner had the castle-clock chimed the hour of midnight, but Edgar sallied from the habitation of cruelty and oppression; nor could the howling wind, the rapid descent of the rain, the vivid flashes of the forked lightning, or the distant crash of the tremendous thunder, induce our hero even to postpone his emprise until a more favourable opportunity; but braving the horrors of the night, before described, until in due time he arrived at the humble cottage occupied by honest Bardolph, on the skirts of the forest.

CHAPTER XI

I see a man's life is a tedious one:
I have tir'd myself;——
Have made the ground my bed. I should be sick,
But that my resolution helps me.

SHAKESPEARE.

EDGAR had retired to rest in the apartment allotted him by Bardolph, and once more the drowsy god of sleep had granted a temporary suspension of tribulation; from which transitory oblivion of misery he was awakened by a violent tumult, which seemed to surround the cottage. Edgar sprang from the bed, and with much expedition hurried on his clothes; this he had hardly completed, when the door below, with great violence, was burst open, and the noise, as of a multitude rushing in, followed immediately after. He heard Bardolph ascend the stairs, and demand the reason of this sudden outrage. At length he distinguished Bernardine's voice, as in reply to Bardolph, loudly exclaim,—

"I am positive, you old scoundrel, he is concealed somewhere about these premises, and I am commanded by Sir Armine to examine every corner of your old hovel; and d—n me, if you presume to obstruct me in performing my duty, I'll set fire to your dirty kennel, and consume your filthy carcase in the midst of it."

Edgar had heard enough to evince himself that he was the innocent cause of this new calamity to poor Bardolph; and dreading, worse than death, a detection which would subject himself again to the tyranny of his uncle, hastily drew back the lattice; and the cottage being very low, leaped from the window upon the turf which surrounded it. The clamour within increased—he knew not where to hide himself—as for many miles around afforded no wood or foliage that would screen him from pursuit. He heard the neighing of horses, and instantly perceived several with their bridles hung loosely over the paling of the cottage: one of these he seized unperceived, as their riders were too much engaged with Bardolph soon to make the discovery: he mounted him and rode off at full speed.

For some time did he gallop on, till the poor beast, almost spent with fatigue, induced him to slacken his pace. He was now on the verge of a thick wood, whose spreading branches were so closely interwoven with each other, as almost intercepted the rays of the sun, which was now rising in all the silent majesty of morning. Here Edgar dismounted, released the bit from the galled mouth of the weary animal, turned his head a contrary road from the one he meant to pursue himself, and sent him off in quest of adventures

Edgar then darted into the thickest part of the wood; and not till being quite tired did he once discontinue his route. At length, quite fatigued, harrassed in body and mind, he sheltered himself beneath the dark foliage of a spreading oak, where he continued until the winged warblers, in clusters, took refuge on the surrounding spray, and with their dulcet evening notes informed him the God of night, in ebon-car, would once more resume his sway, and spread his dusky mantle o'er the world.

The day had proved uncommonly fine; but the advance of evening portrayed symptoms of an approaching tempest; black clouds were gathering in the distant horizon, that entirely secluded an host of twinkling stars which had began to pierce the atmosphere with their refulgent beams.

Edgar arose, and with melancholy steps endeavoured to discover some human habitation, as the cravings of nature at this juncture was too powerful to be resisted; not having received any sustenance since he escaped the vigilance of his pursuers at Bardolph's cottage.

For a considerable time his researches were ineffectual, and he even wished he had suffered himself to have been conducted, by Bernardine, to that fountain of all his misery, castle Fitz-Elmar; when a distant light, breaking through the under-wood, met his view; this he, though not without extreme difficulty in forcing his way through the birch and gorse which grew in vast profusion around, made up to; it proceeded from a small but neat dwelling, situated so amidst the immense timbers which encompassed it, that it was entirely hid from human observation; and had not the light betrayed it, Edgar had never descried the place.

Any situation was preferable to the predicament in which Edgar laboured at this critical period; wherefore, at all hazards, he determined to enter this occult retirement.

CHAPTER XII

———Ere the bat hath flown
His cloister'd flight; ere, to black Hecate's summons,
The shard-born beetle, with his drowsy hums,
Hath rung night's yawning peal, there shall be done
A deed of dreadful note.

SHAKESPEARE.

EDGAR having reached the entrance, commenced a violent knocking at the door, which was instantly opened; at the same time a voice of reproach ejaculated from within,—Zounds, how violently impatient you are to-night! a body can hardly reach the threshold ere you almost shake the house about one's ears. On perceiving our hero she started back (for it was a woman who had so nimbly answered to Edgar's summons) evidently surprised; which sufficiently indicated she expected other company.

Our hero accosted her with great politeness, beseeching her not to be causelessly alarmed, apologized for the trouble he had given her, and informed her that he had lost his way; and happening, by chance, to stumble on her habitation, hoped she would excuse the liberty he had taken, and afford him shelter from the approaching storm.

During the time Edgar was speaking, the woman kept her eyes intently fixed upon him, and with much scrutiny examined his person: when he had finished, she, with much apparent willingness to accommodate him, requested him to walk in, as her house was perfectly at his service.

She conducted him into a neat kitchen, seated him by the side of a blazing fire; and, on Edgar's expressing his hunger, placed before him some cold beef, pickles, eggs, &c. and our hero's stomach being too keen to require much inviting, began the attack with an appetite that would have done honour to the greatest epicure in christendom.

The tempest increased vehemently; Edgar enquired of his hostess if he could be furnished with a bed, as it would be impossible he should again discover his road on such a turbulent night, and was answered in the affirmative, if it would be agreeable to himself to sleep in the room usually occupied by the maid-servant; who, fortunately happened at this juncture to be on a visit to her friends, and would not return that evening. This Edgar readily acquiesced with, when his hostess began to express her apprehension at the long absence of her husband, lest some accident had befallen him; who, she informed Edgar, was employed by Sir Austin Delford, to guard his trees, &c. and for which purpose Sir Austin had built them their small habitation in the centre of the estate, that they might always be on the spot, to prevent depredations which had at times been committed, to the destruction of some of his best timbers.

In this simple narration our hero thought he could distinguish an honest heart. He requested to be shewn to his room, which was immediately complied with. He had been left by himself but a few minutes, when a loud knocking announced the return of his host. Edgar listened gently at the door, being desirous to discover if the husband possessed that genuine hospitality which had prejudiced him in favour of the wife. Our hero started back with horrible surprise, when, in the few words of dreadful import which struck his ear, he recognized the well-known voice of Bernardine.

Well, replied the beldam, as Bernardine entered, have you discovered, dispatched, and rendered secure, the castle runaway? Which salutation was answered by a volley of oaths from Bernardine, cursing his ill-luck, and describing our hero's escape from Bardolph's cottage.

Hush, hush, rejoined the wife, I have him under our roof at this moment.

40

Impossible! thundered Bernardine; would he were, this dagger should drink his blood; he as good as told me, yester-morn, that I was accessary to the murder of ——

Hush, hush, again reiterated this female fiend, we shall disturb him; and the pleasantest method will be to dispatch him when he is asleep.

Hell and furies, are you certain it is Edgar?

Quite certain, replied the hag,—though I never set eyes on him but once before, I am positive I am not mistaken;—however, step into this back room, speak low, and I'll inform you how I have deceived him into security.

They retired into the room, and Edgar heard no more. His situation was terrible—to escape impossible, as the chamber afforded but one small window, and that was strongly barri-caded with rods of iron, which he, on his entrance into the apartment, remarked with a degree of astonishment. One of these, he with much labour wrenched from the casement. Thus armed, he waited the moment of attack, determined to defend himself to the last extremity.

About midnight, the noise of a ladder placed against the wall in the room below, gave notice of the attempt which was about to be made. Soon after a trap-door was gently raised by the side of his bed; he hid himself behind the bed-furniture, and at the instant when Bernardine had half entered the room, he let fall such a tremendous blow on his head with his iron weapon, that he dropped senseless into the apartment from which he had just ascended.

The light being extinguished, the woman, who mistook her wounded husband for our hero, seized hold of him, and as Edgar imagined, gave the finishing stroke, by cutting his throat; then lifting up another trap-door, tumbled the body into a pit concealed beneath it, exclaiming,—There you will find com-pany as taciturn as yourself; what a mercy it is that dead men tell no tales.—Then raising her voice, she called Bernardine, enquiring why he waited. Edgar descended, speaking very low; and, as well as he was able, feigning Bernardine's voice, informed her he must away to the castle, and acquaint the Baron with his success; and in spight of the remonstrance of the hag to postpone his journey until the morning, he, undiscovered, regained the door, darted forward, and once more, 'midst the horrors of the night, found himself bewildered in the gloomy intricate mazes of the wood.

CHAPTER XIII

Now o'er one half the world
Nature seems dead, and wicked dreams abuse
The curtain'd sleep: now witchcraft celebrates
Pale Hecate's offerings; and wither'd Murther,
Alarum'd by his centinel, the wolf,
Whose howl's his watch, thus with his stealthy pace,
With Tarquin's ravishing strides, towards his design
Moves like a ghost.

SHAKESPEARE.

EDGAR pressed forward whichever road chance might direct him, frequently stumbling over the clumps of trees, the trunks of which had been hewn down; but a part of the root still projecting above the earth, rendered walking extremely hazardous, particularly in a night when the intense gloom buried them in obscurity.

About two hours had he continued wandering indiscriminately wherever he could distinguish an opening, his mind totally absorbed in a melancholy retrospect of the occurrences of the evening, when he was suddenly startled from his reverie by the rude shock of some person running violently against him. Edgar retreated a few paces, and in a determined tone, demanded who passed there? Damnation, exclaimed the unknown, sure I should know that voice.—So, so, young gentleman, I have been fortunate enough to light of you at last. A pretty chace you have given us; but you shall now return with me to castle Fitz-Elmar. Edgar would have made his escape, but the ruffian had already griped him by the throat, and bellowed as loudly as his mighty lungs would permit him,— Halloo! Cuthbert, Leonard, Walter, Geoffry, halloo, halloo!—Where are you? Haste, haste, I have him, halloo! This noisy summons was answered by loud shouts from all sides, and

43

Edgar heard them fast approaching. He closed with his antagonist, and had nearly extricated himself from his grasp; the villain thus likely to be overborne, unsheathed his dagger, and with uplifted arm was about to plunge it in Edgar's breast, when, with a sudden jerk, he freed himself from his hold. Another of the party arriving at this critical moment, and endeavouring to seize our hero, received the point of the impending weapon full in his chest: he immediately dropped, and the other, not discovering his error, repeated the stroke. Edgar, much agitated, and having once more baffled the designs of these inhuman monsters, soon got without hearing; and not doubting but as soon as the mistake should be discovered they would again pursue him, he concealed himself in the underwood; but finding all remained silent, again ventured to continue his peregrination. Sometimes he would imagine he heard the sound of distant voices; again he would fly for shelter, and again venture out when everything appeared tranquil.

Thus passed the night.—The storm had subsided, and as bright Sol darted his golden spangles from the eastern horizon, Edgar emerged from the wood, and unmolested continued his route over the most unfrequented paths, till almost the close of day, when, on the declivity of a stupendous mountain, delightfully situated by the margin of a lake which washed its base, in a recess formed by the prolific hand of nature, Edgar, to his unspeakable satisfaction, descried the solitary residence of a hermit.

CHAPTER XIV

For my own part, with resignation still
I can submit to my Creator's will:
Let him recall the breath from him I drew
When he thinks fit, and how he pleases too.
If to the seats of happiness I go,
There end all possible returns of woe:
And when to those blest mansions I arrive,
With pity I'll behold those that survive.

POMFRET.

ON Edgar's arrival at the hermit's abode, the venerable man rose up to receive him, evidently astonished at this unexpected visit.

Edgar, almost fainting with fatigue, *sans ceremonie*, entered the cell, and threw himself on the hard couch which constituted part of its furniture, and in piteous accents lamented his cruel destiny.

The hoary father, with the mild voice of commiseration, endeavoured to sooth his anguish, and benignly enquired the nature of his present calamity, and whether it would admit of mitigation by any means within the compass of his circumscribed power to bestow.

It was long since Edgar had been cheered with the sympathetic sounds of compassion; a pellucid tear of gratitude glistened in his eye. The majestic appearance of the recluse filled him with reverential awe, resignation, and patient endurance, under a multiplicity of ills which diurnally accumulate to harrass and perplex the mind, were indelibly impressed on his features. Edgar scrupled not to relate to him every incident which had occurred to distress him, from the period his father had departed with his sovereign to subdue the infidels, down to

45

the present time: so perfectly was he convinced, at first sight, of the integrity of this august personage.

I see, my son (fervidly exclaimed the hermit when Edgar had finished his recital) the heavy rod of stern oppression is uplifted by the sanguinary hand of Avarice and Murder; and should opportunity convene to aid them in their iniquity, youth and innocence must fall a martyr to the fell machinations of determined villany.

Edgar appeared extremely agitated; when the hermit, gently seizing his hand, continued:—

Yet doubt not, my son, but that omnipresent Power who has hitherto preserved thee, if thou firmly reliest upon him, will still continue to protect thee, and render abortive the dark designs of thine enemies. My residence shall be your sanctuary for the present; here you may remain secure, till fortune appears more inclined to favour you.

Our hero readily embraced the proposal of the recluse; and several weeks had been passed at the hermitage, when one morning, on Edgar's appearing more dejected than usual, his venerable monitor thus addressed him:—

Droop not, my son, beneath the oppressive weight of thy afflictions, nor imagine that thou alone art destined to sip the bitter dregs from the cup of tribulation. Listen to my tale, the distressing vicissitudes of life which I have for many years experienced, and extract the honey of fortitude and resignation from the woe-fraught narration of one who has long since resigned the deluding hope of obtaining happiness in this world; and who patiently waits the blessed reward, which is promised to all true penitents in that which is to come. My misfortunes have been manifold, yet am I enabled to endure them: though I still drag on a weary existence, yet do I not repine, but wait the dread summons of that Supreme Being who gave the vital spark of life to this frail frame of mortality; whose power is infinite, and whose mercy knoweth no bounds.

CHAPTER XV

The ways of Heav'n are dark and intricate;
Puzzled in mazes, and perplex'd with errors.
ADDISON.

DESCENDED from an indigent family in the north of Scotland, whose daily toils hardly procured sustenance for a numerous progeny. I was about nine years of age when a worthy gentleman, merely through compassion for my father, took me under his protection, put me out to school, so that what little erudition I have acquired has been entirely owing to his bounty. With him I quitted my native land: and in all the vividness of youth and innocence, arrived safe with him at his house in London. The first two years of my life, after I quitted the school, I was employed, by my benefactor, in the capacity of foot-boy; who, finding me grateful for his favours, and attentive to every part of my vocation, promoted me to a more exalted station in his household. Suffice it to say, that after about twenty years had expired, from the date I quitted Scotland, during which time I had been placed in business by the beneficent hand of my master, I found myself in possession of near five thousand marks, which was hourly accumulating. I paid my addresses to a citizen's daughter of large property; my suit was willingly admitted by the parents; Alethea smiled propitious on my love, and Hymen crowned our wishes.

Five thousand angels I received the day after our marriage, as my wife's dowery; and in the space of five years, from our nuptials, my wealth was considerably increased—with one son and two daughters.

So totally was I absorbed in devising methods still to improve my fortune, that I never dreamed of my poor relations in Scotland; that is, I never dreamed of alleviating their misery,

47

by diminishing their necessities: this was inimical to my system of improvement; and I more than once rejected the supplication of my father, who had heard of my affluence, and had written to me for pecuniary assistance: avarice at that time had so steeled my breast, that I would almost have parted with life in preference to a mark. But that Being who had prospered me in my endeavours, and loaded me with riches that I might assist the unfortunate and relieve the indigent, severely punished me for this abuse of his goodness, and reduced me, from being one of the happiest and most opulent of men in the metropolis of England, to one of the most miserable.

A young gentleman, of good family, requested my permission to pay his devoirs to my eldest daughter; but his fortune being small, I peremptorily rejected his overture, and dismissed him from my presence with every term of reproach I was master of for his presumption; though, at the same time, I was acquainted that he was tenderly beloved by my child; but my heart was callous to the misery in which I had plunged my family by my cruel inflexibility. My wife, on her knees, intreated for her Emily; but it was all to no purpose, Mammon was the deity to whom I daily addressed my obsecrations; in him I trusted for happiness in this world: and wofully was I disappointed.

However, I obstinately persisted in my determination never to sanction their nuptials with my approbation; and in a few weeks after, this young gentleman sailed for the West Indies to take possession of a small estate which had been recently bequeathed to him by a friend deceased, from whence he never returned; change of climate did not agree with him, together with an extreme melancholy which had seized his heretofore volatile disposition, preyed upon his constitution, that in a few weeks after he quitted England, he was no more.—I had heard of his dissolution with ecstasy: but who can paint my rage when my wife informed me that my daughter was pregnant! I was transfixed with horror — my blood boiled in my veins — and for some time I lost the power of articulation. However, having a little overcome my first astonishment, I hurried into my daughter's apartment, seized her by the hair of her head, and with violent execrations, turned her into the street; and notwithstanding the heart-rending shrieks and prayers of my wife, banished her from my dwelling, without the means to purchase the common necessaries of life.

My son I had placed at the university at Oxford; but my accursed thirst for gold had so contracted my heart, that I refused to remit him those requisite supplies, so indispensably necessary to keep him on a footing with his fellow compeers. The consequence was, he was detected in a forgery, tried, condemned, and executed!

My cruelty to my daughter had almost broken my wife's heart; but this last stroke was more than her tender nature could bear; and six days after the execution of my son, she resigned her soul into the hands of her Creator.

It was now that I began to perceive the atrocity of my conduct. My wife I tenderly loved, and, notwithstanding my rigid behaviour, I doated on my son. A violent fever seized my brain; and for many weeks I lay in the most alarming state of insensibility, that life seemed tottering on the brink of eternity. I however at last recovered; but so perfectly altered in my disposition, that could the whole of my fortune have purchased the happiness I had lost, without a murmur I had parted with it; but Providence ordained it otherwise; I was not yet sufficiently punished for my crimes. On my recovery, I caused every possible research to be made after my daughter, whom I had so inhumanly driven from my protection; and at last discovered her, loaded with disease and rags, and nearly perishing for want of bread. She had been decoyed into the dwelling of a common procuress, there delivered of a dead child, as my violent treatment of her had caused a premature labour; and the mother being such whose person would suit the wretch who had thus timely rescued her from destruction, informed her the only remaining way of repaying the obligation. The poor girl had no other alternative than either to accede to the bawd's proposal, or again encounter the pinching gripe of penury, a miserable victim in the public streets, so that necessity, not principle, obliged her to agree to every thing this hell-born imp of iniquity requested, till time and disease once more drove her upon the town, helpless and alone; in which distressed situation I at length discovered her. I took her home with me, behaved to her with the affection of a parent, kindly obduced her indiscretions, and my mind regained some little degree of composure.

My other daughter grew jealous of my attention to her sister; and, whenever I was absent, would reproach her for her imprudence, with every bitter epithet that envy or malignancy could suggest.

One evening, after repeated insults of this kind, Emily, unknown to any one, quitted my house, and in the river terminated a life rendered wretched by the atrocious conduct of an unfeeling father.

This shocking catastrophe again reduced me to the brink of the grave; and scarcely had I attained to a state of convalescence, when my other daughter, my only surviving child, was taken from me by a fall from her horse.

Thus was I bereft of all my children; myself only left, a mournful example to the avaricious and unfeeling.

I dispatched an express into Scotland to my parents, remitting a sufficient supply of money to defray their expences, requesting their immediate presence in London. But alas they were no more! they sickened at the inhumanity of their child, and, not being able to pursue their accustomed vocations, died for the want of food.

However, three brothers, the sole survivors of my unhappy family, in Scotland, quickly obeyed my summons: to them I made over near the whole of my immense possessions, reserving for myself but a very moderate portion of cash, in case of absolute necessity.

I quitted London unknown to any one; and after a wearysome journey of some days, discovered this solitary recess. Twenty years have I inhabited it; and, though I have still money at command, yet have I persevered in the most extreme forbearance. My food has been the roots of the earth, my drink the water from the crystal stream: and here will I linger the remainder of my days, till that Being, whom I have so justly offended, is satisfied with my contrition, has sealed my pardon for my manifold transgressions, and extinguished the spark of life, only that it may blaze with divine refulgency in a blessed eternity.

CHAPTER XVI

To extinguish bad passions, and to regulate good
ones, are the two great points within the compass
of our reason.

PRATT.

HERE the anchorite finished his tale, and retired to compose the
tempest in his mind the painful recital of his calamities had
excited.

Edgar felt himself comparatively happy; for though he had
been of late extremely buffetted by the wayward gales of
outrageous fortune, his mind was not contaminated by any
events occurring through the medium of vicious and ungovern-
able propensities.

His conscience reproached him not; and could he but
possess his dear Helen, unmolested by his sanguinary uncle, his
past misfortunes had been swallowed in the gulf of oblivion;
and a cottage, with the moderate requisites of existence, had
been the summit of his ambition, and himself of course unchangeably happy.

Such was Edgar's present reflections; so diametrically
opposite to the sentiments of an eminently celebrated and very
justly admired author, who has given it as his opinion, that

Man soon tires of every thing in this life; riches are a burthen
to the possessor; ambition, when sated, leaves regrets; the
sweets of love lose their pleasure;—and, upon the whole, that
mankind are born to live either in the distraction of inquie-
tude, or in the lethargy of disgust.

However, Edgar was possessed of too volatile a disposition
to meditate deeper than appeared congruous to what might

afford present enjoyment: and could he but obtain that, his ideas never extended to the possibility of an alteration.

Several months elapsed, and Edgar continued residentiary at the Hermitage. He became more pensive; no creature had visited the retreat since his arrival; nor had he even descried a human figure at a distance, save his guardian-angel in the venerable form of the anchorite; and each revolving day passed monotonously away.

Edgar became anxious to learn the state of affairs at Castle Fitz-Elmar since he had fled from it, and whether his Helen still was with his uncle, or if her brother had as yet made his appearance, and taken her under his protection.

Several weeks more passed away in the same tranquil manner as the preceding, ere Edgar could summon sufficient courage to quit his asylum; when he informed the hermit of his intention to return to Bardolph's cottage; at the same time remarking, that should the Baron still persevere in his endeavours to discover his refuge, Bardolph's habitation would be the least liable again to excite suspicion, as all apprehension that he would venture to sanctuarize himself so near the castle must long ere this have ceased, must have been totally resigned as fallacious and improbable.

The recluse at first attempted to persuade Edgar to defer his journey for a few weeks longer, as he was most firmly of opinion that it would be impossible he should gain the skirts of the forest without being discovered by some of the Baron's emissaries: but perceiving Edgar hurt by his advice, he reluctantly acquiesced; and the day succeeding, Edgar prepared to depart, when his hoary monitor thus addressed him:—

Farewell, my son! since I find that I cannot easily persuade thee to continue with me a little longer.—It is my most earnest wish that thou mayest safely, and without the least molestation, reach the place of thy destination.—On every occasion thro' life, let it be your invariable maxim to place a firm confidence and trust in that most benignant and adorable Being, the supreme Creator of all things; and you may confidently rest assured that your hope will not fall to the ground: his aid never fails: he will with safety deliver thee out of the power of thine enemies; and remember, when once thou hast sullied thy good name, by suffering thy principles to degenerate, the sting of remorse will probe thy breast in the hours of retirement. An honest heart is a jewel not to be purchased by the wealth of nations; be careful then to govern thy passions, and preserve thine from the destructive contamination of guilt; persevere in virtue, and merit the commendation of Heaven.

END OF THE FIRST VOLUME.

EDGAR;

OR, THE

PHANTOM OF THE CASTLE

CHAPTER XVII

Good things of Day begin to droop and drowze;
While Night's black agents to their prey do rouse.
                                                    SHAKESPEARE.

EDGAR pursued his journey without encountering any disagreeable incident; and, about two hours after sun-set stopped at a small house, as the letters on the door announced it to have been erected for the accommodation of travellers. Here he undisturbed passed the night. The next morning he recommenced his route, and towards the close of the day arrived at the spot where stood the remains of the humble, but hospitable mansion of his friend Bardolph.

But how altered in appearance since the vile agents of his cruel persecutor, Sir Armine Fitz-Elmar, had obliged him to fly from it.

The cottage now was nothing more than an uncouth heap of rubbish. The grass-plot which surrounded it, and which had ever been preserved in good order by the indefatigable industry of its honest possessor, was black and withered; and in many places entirely gone.

The poplars and shrubs that shaded its entrance, and obstructed the intense heat of the sun in the dry part of the year, when its piercing rays would have incommoded its inhabitants, were likewise destroyed.

An observer, less interested than was Edgar, would have perceived every ostensible reason to conclude, that the desolation around had been occasioned by fire; and, in all human probability its occupiers might have perished in the conflagration.

Edgar contemplated the devastation with horror and astonishment.

Surely, said Edgar to himself, Bardolph cannot thus have been reduced by those damned atrocious miscreants, in revenge for my escape from——Impossible!—I'll not imagine it—the thought is torture.—Poor unfortunate Bardolph, it matters little what occasioned thy calamity, thy sufferings will be hardly less acute did they originate in unavoidable casualty or premeditated villany.

Edgar walked dejectedly away, hardly knowing where he wandered; nor did he, indeed, give himself time to consider, until he found himself within a few paces of the old ruin of the castle, recorded in the first chapter of this history.

The day had now entirely disappeared, and the night, though not tempestuous, was excessively dark.

Edgar shuddered as he beheld the gloomy structure, almost concealed by the darker shades of evening. What he had formerly seen and experienced there, recurred to his memory. He turned from it with an emotion of horror, and was hastening away, when an indescribable impulse again to explore the interior parts of it, arrested his speed, and he again advanced towards it—again his courage failed him, and he retreated:—a third time he changed his resolution and proceeded, with perturbed paces, in a direction to the entrance—again stopped, much agitated, irresolute, and undetermined.

An intuitive impulse at last prevailed. He heard the trampling of horses; they might be his enemies: he with quickness ascended the stone steps, and found himself at the very door which had admitted him into the building on a former occasion.

CHAPTER XVIII

What awful silence! How these antique towers
And vacant courts chill the suspended soul!
Till Expectation wears the face of Fear;
And Fear, half ready to become Devotion,
Mutters a kind of mental orison,
It knows not wherefore—What a kind of being
Is Circumstance!

HORACE WALPOLE.

ON Edgar's pressing against the door, it opened, as before. With the slightest difficulty he entered, and closed it gently after him, that the secret springs which held it fast when shut with violence, might not again retard his escape, should circumstances render it necessary; as he conjectured the wind, forcing a passage through the mouldering walls, had before effected what he now endeavoured to prevent.

He groped his way, and soon regained the staircase he had formerly descended, pursued the same pass, entered by the iron door, and found himself in the square room, the incongruities of which had before excited his amazement.

The lamp, which he had seized, and resigned as soon as the light became extinguished, was replaced in its old situation: This he once more possessed himself of, followed the winding passage in the same direction as before, and soon arrived at the door of the room which he had on his first visit burst open. This he again discovered to be firmly secured on the inside; he imagined he heard a murmuring noise, as of a confusion of voices speaking very low; he listened gently—a bolt of the door he distinctly heard moved cautiously back by some person within—he hurried with much terror and precipitancy, into a dark avenue, which the lamp he held made visible to him. This he followed for some time, then turned into another pass, which seemed to wind its course, without any impediment, almost entirely round the edifice; this he likewise quitted, and ascended a few broken steps which appeared in a nook in the wall, shoved open a door which presented itself on their summit, and, to his infinite amazement, found himself within a few paces of the door through which he had at first entered the structure.

Edgar's resolution began to fail him; and having again reached the entrance of the ruin in such a miraculous manner, he almost conceived it to be a supernatural warning for himself immediately to depart.

He hesitated; and though his heart palpitated with fear, curiosity was not yet satisfied. He listened—all was hushed— the most profound silence prevailed around; not a sound was heard, save the moping owl, shrieking dismally from the dreary ruins, which heightened the solemnity of his situation.

His attention was engaged, as he raised the lamp, to observe the place where he then was: it was the remains of a spacious hall, entirely decorated with portraits, large as life, of the august personages who had been its former possessors.

He began to examine the paintings, most of which were mucid, and nearly dropping to decay, as the large gaps in many parts of the structure, at times had exposed them to the rude peltings of the hurricane.

While he was thus employed, he was suddenly alarmed by a noise, as of the rattling together of some heavy pieces of iron. He listened in trembling silence, when a portrait he had been intently gazing at, was torn with violence from its frame, and a heavy weight, with horrid crash, fell almost at his feet.

Mute with horror he stood aghast, expecting nothing less than the immediate destruction of the whole fabric, and himself crushed to atoms in its tremendous fall.

All was again hushed in silence, when, gathering courage from despair, he stooped to examine what it was which had thus excited his unpleasant emotions, and discovered it only to be an old armour, which had been placed in a niche in the wall, and the painting being placed before it, had concealed it from his sight. The support, most likely, on which it rested, being rotten gave way, and dropping forward, the picture which secluded it, was demolished in its descent.

Eternal Providence! Who can describe the sensations of Edgar, when on examining the casque he immediately recognized it to be the same his father wore when he departed with his king to subdue the infidels!

Having again recovered his composure, he proceeded to search the armour, not doubting but that was his father's likewise; nor was he mistaken; the initials which he discovered on the breast-plate (E.F-E.) confirmed it, beyond the probability of deception.

He was determined, be the consequences what they might, if possible to secure it; and scarcely knowing what he did, he hurried it upon himself: this he had hardly effected, when he heard the sound of footsteps approaching, and before he had time to make his escape, his uncle, Sir Armine Fitz-Elmar, to his unspeakable astonishment, entered the hall.

On perceiving our hero thus accoutred in his father's armour, the Baron became convulsed with terror, and uttering a piercing shriek, fell lifeless into the arms of some persons who accompanied him.

Edgar taking advantage of their consternation, darted precipitately into the first pass he descried, and was once more entangled in the intricate avenues leading to the interior apartments of the mouldering priory.

CHAPTER XIX

The wind is up: hark how it howls! methinks
Till now, I never heard a sound so dreary:
Doors creak, and windows clap, and Night's foul bird,
Rook'd in the spire, screams loud.

BLAIR.

EDGAR, immersed in a croud of painful reflections by the strange appearance Sir Armine Fitz-Elmar had excited, passed through a magnificent arcade, which was likewise in many places crumbling to ruin; and entered upon a long gallery, which seemed to lead to a more remote range of apartments, when looking round he discovered a spacious staircase, tottering in superb decay, which, even now, appeared in proud magnificence, and informed every observer what the fabric once had been.

This, with great caution he ascended, as many of the marble steps were loose and broken, and entered upon another gallery which wound its course round the northern wing of the priory. This he pursued, and had nearly gained a door which terminated it, when he stumbled over a heap of rubbish which he was too much agitated to perceive; the lamp flew from his trembling grasp, and he was once more involved in total darkness.

His destruction now appeared inevitable, by means of the frightful chasms in the floor, which he had already with difficulty avoided. Should he turn back, it would be impossible he could escape in the dark; and to proceed farther on, was, in all human conjecture, equally dangerous.

He gave himself up for lost, when, despondently turning his head, he discovered a ray of light issuing from an half-closed door in an obscure corner of the gallery, which faintly gleaming on the ruins, enabled him to reach the apartment from whence it was emitted; and softly moving back the door, beheld—(merciful Heaven!)—entering from an opposite pass of the chamber, a form whom he imagined to be no longer in existence—killed by his own hand—the hideous, the sanguinary, the inhuman Bernardine!

An universal trembling seized his frame; almost fainting he reclined against the wall, and gasped for breath.

Nor did Bernardine appear less completely terrified on descrying Edgar: for some moments he was transfixed to the spot. His lips quivered, and his knees knocked together, when he in tremulous accents, scarcely audible, pronounced, "Merciful Father, hide me from the sight of that horrid spectre! vouchsafe to accept the prayer of a penitent, and—Oh! save me, save me!"—He could articulate no more; he dropped senseless on the floor in a seeming agony of remorse for the horrid crimes with which his guilty head was loaded.

At the same instant two ruffians burst into the apartment, seized on Edgar, more dead than alive, firmly bound him with cords, and, without uttering a syllable, bore him between them, through many intricate passes and gloomy avenues, till reaching the chapel, which was contiguous to the eastern wing of the priory, traversed the gloomy aisles of the solemn structure; and having gained its centre, descended by a trap-door into a vault beneath, first securing the entrance with much apparent caution after them.

CHAPTER XX

I'll tell thee what, my friend,
He is a very serpent in my way;
And wheresoe'er this foot of mine doth tread,
He lies before me.

SHAKESPEARE.

IT is now time we should return to castle Fitz-Elmar, and learn what had passed there since Edgar had deserted it.

His escape was not discovered until the family were assembled round the breakfast-table; when his not attending, as customary, informed the guilty mind of the Baron the occasion of his absence.

Lucretia, bursting into tears and violent reproaches, not unaccompanied with gross invectives, levelled her upbraidings at the beautiful Helen; who, though previously acquainted of Edgar's departure, was much affected; and the torrent of abuse bestowed upon her by Lucretia, made her hastily retire from the breakfast-hall, and endeavoured to compose her much agitated spirits in her own apartment.

The Baron, on being informed that Edgar was nowhere to be found, started from his chair—every feature was convulsed with rage—when clenching his hands and striking them with violence on the table, with horrid imprecations, vowed dire vengeance on his innocent nephew, should he once more have him within the gripe of his power.

The castle was now in the most violent uproar; while, old Conrad, the domestic before mentioned, who had been entrusted with the care of the castle in the absence of the family, and who was firmly attached to Edgar, inwardly exulted in his escape,

"Smil'd in the tumult, and enjoy'd the storm."

63

Bernardine was then immediately summoned to attend Sir Armine in the library, his usual resort when he had any secret work of iniquity to be performed by this diabolical, but trusty, agent in his wickedness.

This conference did not continue long, when Bernardine, with the major part of the domestics, were dispatched (mounted on the best horses the Baron's stud afforded) different roads, if possible to overtake Edgar, and reconduct him to castle Fitz-Elmar.

The night was far advanced ere these unsuccessful tools of oppression returned; when Bernardine first suggested to the Baron the probability that Edgar had sanctuarized himself in Bardolph's cottage.

Conviction flashed on Sir Armine's mind as he with much fervour exclaimed, "I have not a doubt but he is there at this instant; haste, fly, my good Bernardine, threaten the villain into compliance, should you find it necessary; nay, more—you understand me, Bernardine—respecting Edgar, I have before given you my instructions—rid me of this plague and your fortune's made—be vigilant and also secret. How truly unfortunate that our hurry this morning should make me forget what, of all other places in our present predicament, I ought to have remembered; but my dear Bernardine, use every possible dispatch, and return as early as the business will permit, and acquaint me of your success."

Bernardine bowed submission, remounted his horse, and rode off to execute the commission of his wicked employer.

CHAPTER XXI

I have done a thousand dreadful things,
As willingly as one would kill a fly;
Acts of black night, abominable deeds,
Complots of mischief, treason; villanies
Ruthful to hear, yet piteously perform'd.

SHAKESPEARE.

TO inform the reader why the Baron placed so much confidence in Bernardine, it is requisite he should know the adventure which first introduced them to each other.

Soon after, the Baron arrived at castle Fitz-Elmar, apparently agreeable to Sir Edgar's letter; but in fact, with no other motive than to secure his brother's wealth to himself, by hiring some bravos to waylay and assassinate him.

But whom to employ to perpetrate this deed, was no difficult point to determine; he would not have hesitated to have done it himself, but he had not the courage; and even if he had, Sir Edgar, he well knew, would be attended by Bardolph; and more than one person must be hired, in consequence, to assist him.

One evening, having wandered a considerable distance from the castle, totally absorbed in these gloomy reflections—that the setting sun had shed his golden spangles from the western horizon, and the dusky tints of evening were fast approaching, ere he discovered he had advanced so far; he hastily turned himself, and was shaping his course toward the castle, when an unknown person, who had been concealed behind a clump of trees, made up to him, held a poniard to his breast, and demanded, as he valued his life, his money.

Sir Armine, trembling with fear, emptied his pockets into the robber's hand, who willingly received its golden contents, and was eagerly making off with his booty, when the Baron,

65

somewhat recovered from his first surprize, summoned the villain to return; for he had an idea that the promise of more gold might induce the ruffian to perpetrate the act he had been so many days puzzling his brain, to no purpose, whom to employ.

The man at first hesitated; but observing all quiet around, and the Baron unarmed, he, with much ferocity of aspect, his poniard unsheathed, ready to defend himself should circumstances render it necessary, returned, and demanded an explanation of Sir Armine's conduct.

Suffice it to observe, that the Baron found him every thing he wished him; and before they parted, he ventured to inform him his name and place of abode; and the ruffian finding him thus explicit, acquainted Sir Armine that he belonged to a numerous gang of banditti, whose general rendezvous was the old ruin on the forest, and that he might depend on his commands being executed with the profoundest secresy, punctuality, and dispatch.

Sir Armine was overjoyed—he wished to have farther converse with him—but as public meetings might create suspicion, he agreed to receive him at the castle; and to prevent impertinent remarks, made him one of his household; and that his absence from the castle should not be subject to the observation of the residentiaries there, he assigned him the office of watchman: in which character he on the subsequent evening appeared in *propria personæ.*

Sir Edgar Fitz-Elmar, as before expressed, fell a victim to their villany: and Bernardine, for it was himself, finding his place lucrific, was true to the Baron's interest, and at his request, continued his nocturnal occupation, ever ready to assist in any nefarious undertaking, when it would be dangerous a more honest person should be employed.

Sir Armine finding, by the obstinacy and escape of his nephew, that a few months might dispossess him of the immense property which he held in trust for him, privately informed Bernardine, that if he and his confederates would undertake to rid him of Edgar in like manner as they had done his father, the reward for the second assassination should more than doubly exceed what they had received for the first.

Bernardine cheerfully complied, and as readily answered for the acquiescence of his associates.

This once effected, every thing the Baron held in trust for Edgar, as expressed by his brother's will, in case his son did not survive his minority, should devolve to his daughter Lucretia.

This commission was not given to Bernardine until after the fruitless research of the domestics, when he rode off from the castle—soon gained Bardolph's cottage—and the reception he met with there (as expressed in the third chapter) so strengthened his suspicion, that Edgar had placed himself under Bardolph's protection: he immediately joined the banditti on the forest, informed them of the nature of his present engagement, and in a very short time after, himself, and ten of the most desperate of the gang, found themselves at the entrance of Bardolph's cottage.

CHAPTER XXII

All pow'rful gold with influence doth win
Men, with desire for to engender sin.

GOFFE.

To prevent Edgar's escaping, should he really have secreted himself in Bardolph's cottage, Bernardine deemed it most expedient that the whole of the troop should dismount, secure their horses to the fence of the cottage, and without giving Bardolph any notice of their arrival, to break into his dwelling, and, *sans ceremonie*, search every part of it.

This was no sooner determined than carried into execution. The door was presently shattered to atoms, and the whole of the gang immediately entered. Bardolph, much alarmed, arose at the noise; and Edgar effected his escape from the window, as described in Chapter XI. Vol. I.

Bardolph was too soon made acquainted with their intentions, and would have prevented the villains from ascending the stairs, for which purpose he seized his trusty sabre, freed it from the scabbard, and placed himself in a posture of defence; but was soon overpowered and disarmed.

Old Dorothy, who had been screaming with affright and apprehension for her husband's life, was forcibly dragged from her apartment, and was, with honest Bardolph, thrust out of the cottage with violent execrations from Bernardine, that if either of them presumed to enter it before he had satisfied himself whether Edgar was, or was not concealed there, that moment should be their last.

The apartments were examined minutely; a miniature picture was found in one of them, which Bernardine immediately knew to be Edgar's: this was an indubitable proof that their suspicions were not fallacious; the window likewise being

68

open, and the lattice for the most part destroyed, conveyed to him the means of his escape; he descended the stairs with much haste, and was soon on the exterior of the cottage, well convinced, in his own mind, that should Edgar have descended from the window, as he firmly believed he had, he must soon be within their power, as the barren waste, for many miles around, could not screen him from their warm pursuits.

But who can delineate his passion and surprize when he discovered in what manner our hero had eluded his vigilance! Bardolph had certainly fallen a victim to the first impulse of his passion, but, fortunately for him, he had with extreme pleasure obtained a glimpse of Edgar as he furiously rode off on one of the villain's horses; and having every thing to fear from the brutal rage of his baffled pursuers, he and old Dorothy made the best of their way over the dreary waste of the forest.

Bernardine, as a reward for the duplicity of Bardolph, ordered his cottage to be set on fire; which being accomplished, they sallied forth in quest of their prey.

The animal on which Edgar had so fortunately escaped, was met by Bernardine and his followers. This was accounted a lucky incident, as it informed them the object of their search could not be far off.

They soon gained the wood in which Edgar lay concealed; this they agreed accurately to examine, for which purpose they dismounted, secured their horses to the trees, and began their search.

Had not Edgar continued on the spot where fatigue first induced him to throw himself, he must inevitably have fallen into their hands, for Bernardine planted his colleagues so judiciously in different situations, that it was impossible for any person who passed to escape their observation.

The whole of the day did they continue their fruitless search, and were farther determined still to persevere the whole of the night, being convinced, to a man, that Edgar had concealed himself in some obscure part of the wood; and if they continued indefatigable in their search, it would be impossible he should long remain undiscovered.

The evening was dark and tempestuous; Bernardine, heartily tired, summoned part of his followers, and advised them, as they hoped to partake of a good round sum of money for their labour, to be vigilant, while he retired to give some requisite instructions to black Mary at their occasional rendezvous; and should they have any occasion for him before he returned, he was there to be found.

CHAPTER XXIII

I have almost forgot the taste of fears:
The time has been, my senses would have cool'd
To hear a night-shriek; and my fell hair
Would at a dismal treatise rouse and stir
As life were in't: I have supp'd full with horrors;
Direness, familiar to my slaught'rous thoughts,
Cannot once start me.

SHAKESPEARE.

THIS rendezvous was no other than that mysterious building in which Edgar had sheltered himself from the increasing vehemence of the storm: erected in a part of the wood almost rendered inaccessible by its being totally hemmed in by trees, whose spreading branches, so closely interwoven with each other, screened it from the enquiring gaze of the curious traveller.

This structure had been contrived by Bernardine, as a most eligible retreat where they could retire to in time of danger, or devise mischief for the better support of their nefarious avocations.

For some time after Bernardine had quitted his companions, did they, with unremitting diligence, continue their allotted tasks, until the rude pelting of the pityless storm obliged them to suspend their examination until the raging tempest a little subsided.

This determined, they were hastening to join Bernardine at their rendezvous; when one of the banditti, who had advanced some few paces forwarder than the rest, alarmed the gang with loud and repeated shouts for assistance; the villains, obedient to his summons, were soon up with him; and finding him grappling with a person whom he affirmed to be Edgar, one of them immediately unsheathed a dagger—but the intense darkness

71

rendering it impossible for him to discriminate his object, he lodged the deadly point, intended for Edgar, in his comrade's breast: he fell, and the uplifted weapons of the others, who were by this time arrived on the spot, quickly dispatched him.

Joy at their success filled the minds of each, and loud shouts of exultation resounded through the gloomy avenues of the wood, as they bore the bleeding corpse towards their rendezvous.

Black Mary was at the door to receive them, and conceiving the body which they supported had been some unfortunate traveller whom they had robbed and murdered (too much used to such spectacles to discover any token of surprize now) she threw open the receptacle, usual on such occasions, and was proceeding to inform them of the assassination of Edgar by herself and Bernardine; and gave in her claim as entitled to a considerable portion of the reward.

Why, what the devil is the old woman bothering us about? exclaimed one of them—yourself and Bernardine completed the job—you entitled to a considerable part of the reward! Be easy, old woman; and when next you are to appear before your betters, be sure you keep yourself sober.

Here a battle would certainly have commenced, for black Mary had already clenched her fists and placed herself in an attitude suitable to her intentions, vociferating, as there was no other system which she could adopt so effectually to evince him of her integrity than by beating it into his mud-stuffed skull, why, she would e'en submit to the necessity of the times, and chastise him in a manner his insolence merited; but the gang interfering, for this time prevented the contest.

Black Mary, a little appeased by the persuasive eloquence of Hubert, who had been particularly active in endeavouring to stop the current of abuse which was gathering, and would soon have overwhelmed the unanimity of the whole party but for his timely interference, was preparing to convey the body to the old place of interment, when she discovered the distorted visage of Hugo in the bloodstained corpse stretched out before her.

She started back, and with a yell of horror, exclaimed, O ye infernal brutes! what! treacherous even to yourselves!—and is poor Hugo fallen a victim to your damned contrivances!—Oh! bloody, bloody savages!

The scene which followed this discovery, is easier conceived than expressed; rage and astonishment was depicted on every countenance, and the particulars of this unfortunate catastrophe was recited to black Mary, who, on hearing that Hugo met with his death by accident, and not through any premeditated treachery of his companions, was soon reconciled to the event; but that they should meet with Edgar in the wood, exceeded her belief; and she briefly gave them the history of his assassination, perpetrated by herself and Bernardine.

Here black Mary received the loud rebukes of the whole gang; and blows would certainly have followed, had not Hubert again quelled the dispute, by offering to descend the cavern.— And if Edgar is certainly dispatched as old Mary peremptorily affirms he is, I will return with the body, that you may all have ocular demonstration of the fact; for I find, oral testimony will never prove sufficient to convince any of us.

This was no sooner proposed than adopted. Hubert descended the cavern, and returned soon after, not with the body of Edgar, but, to their extreme confusion, the hideous carcase of Bernardine.

Black Mary stood aghast—a trembling seized her limbs as she contemplated the bloody scene before her; many times was she interrogated by the astonished group ere she could sufficiently compose herself to give an answer, when she again endeavoured to explain the occurrences of the evening; when Hubert, from the lame account she gave, and conceiving, by her being so much agitated, that she alone had reduced Bernardine to so deplorable a situation,—he, with one stroke of his sabre, separated her head from her shoulders, and tumbled her withered trunk into the pit, to fill up the vacancy, occupied but a few minutes previously by Bernardine.

On examining Bernardine, who by long and repeated groans evinced them he was not yet dead, they discovered a violent contusion on the left part of his head; his shoulder was likewise much lacerated; for black Mary, in her hurry to dispatch him, had placed her instrument rather lower than she intended.

It was the general opinion that Bernardine's wounds were not mortal, and that if they could convey him to the castle and place him under the protection of the Baron, he would soon procure him such assistance as would in a short time restore him to himself; and that they ought for the present to postpone their search after Edgar, and give all their attention to their wounded friend.

This point being fixed, they conveyed him, under cover of the night, to that mansion of oppression, castle Fitz-Elmar.

CHAPTER XXIV

A greater Pow'r than we can contradict,
Hath thwarted our intents.

SHAKESPEARE.

THE raging violence of the storm subsided as the ruddy tints of morning glowed in the east; the feathered songsters once more in clusters sought the happy spray, and with their dulcet notes melodiously welcomed the rising lamp of day. Millions of aromatic shrubs, almost annihilated by the late tempest, raised their drooping heads, and embalmed with their odoriferous exhalations, the breath of Morn. The fleecy tribe, in merry antics gambolled o'er the swelling turf; the horrors of the night was lost in oblivion, and cheerfulness seemed to reign predominant throughout the enchanting landscape.

Sir Armine Fitz-Elmar, eager to make enquiries respecting the success of Bernardine, now quitted his apartment, where he had tremblingly passed the night; the dreadful stings of conscience had, long since, made retirement irksome, and this night, in particular, had been attended with more than its usual proportion of horrors; thrice had his guilty mind conjured up to his tortured fancy, the bleeding image of his murdered brother, as he lay convulsed in fear, and shivering with apprehension, lest every crash of thunder, which seemed bursting over his head, was winged from Heaven to hurl his guilty soul into everlasting perdition.

With much trepidation, therefore, on the first appearance of day-light he descended into the hall, where Conrad informed him that Bernardine had been robbed, and nearly murdered by some ruffians in the forest; that he had some time since been conveyed to his chamber, put to bed, and in all human probability by this time he was no more; one of the honest gentlemen who conducted him home, continued Conrad, gave me this letter to deliver into your hands.

The Baron received the letter, and, with evident perturbation, read as follows:

To Sir Armine Fitz-Elmar.

"I am sorry to inform you, Sir, that our utmost endeavours have been without effect; Edgar yet lives; thrice we had him almost within our grasp, and thrice has he rendered our schemes abortive. Where he is now, Heaven only knows. Take care of Bernardine—we imagine he received his wounds from Edgar, who shall not long enjoy his triumph. We are stimulated now by a double motive;—interest and revenge. Bardolph we have likewise punished for his treachery towards us, but not sufficiently. Ere to-morrow's rising sun proclaims another day, expect to hear of the dissolution of both.

Yours sincerely,

HUBERT."

The Baron, on reading the contents of this epistle, ordered Conrad to shew him into Bernardine's apartment. On his entering the room, Bernardine no sooner observed him than he deliriously exclaimed, "Ha! what thou art come to take the blame upon thyself—to clear me of that load of guilt which else will sink my soul into everlasting darkness."—Then fixing his eyes in a vacant stare, he continued—"Behold that horrid

phantom there—Oh! shake not your gory locks at me.—O! Sir
Edgar, 'twas your brother's cursed gold induced me to do the
deed; shower down thy hottest vengeance on his head who first
suggested—— See! See! he comes this way—save me from his
gripe—oh! mercy, save me, save me!"

Bernardine, entirely exhausted by this violent exertion,
once more dropped lifeless on his pillow; every faculty seemed
suspended; the icy hand of Death seemed to have extinguished
the vital spark of existence.

The Baron was rivetted to the spot with horror, till a deep
groan from Bernardine aroused him; he staggered a few paces
from the bed and gasped for breath.

The surgeon, and the few domestics who were present, were
mute with astonishment, when the Baron suddenly recovering,
darted out of the room, and was followed by Conrad. Having
gained the hall, too much overcome by his fears, and not
doubting but Bernardine in his delirium would betray every
thing he knew, almost fainting he threw himself into a chair,
and groaned dreadfully aloud.

Conrad flew to his assistance. The Baron started with alarm
at the sound of his voice, but on perceiving who it was, again
dropped into the chair, and in the anguish of his mind the
scalding tears of remorse trickled down his face; but, alas! this
remorse was of short duration, for soon recovering his equanimity, and with it also his accustomed habitual ferocity, he sternly
commanded Conrad to retire, and no more to obtrude himself
where his presence was not required.

CHAPTER XXV

The night has been unruly. Where we lay,
Our chimnies were blown down: and, as they say,
Lamentings heard i'the air; strange screams of death;
And prophesying, with accents terrible,
Of dire combustion, and confus'd events,
New hatch'd to the woful time: The obscure bird
Clamour'd the live-long night: some say, the earth
Was ferverous, and did shake.

SHAKESPEARE.

CONRAD was about to obey him, but was prevented by a sudden and violent crash, which shook the castle to its very base. The Baron started with affright, and with trembling accent, commanded Conrad not to depart. Immediately after, to their utter astonishment, Helen entered the hall, her countenance pallid with extreme fear, her hair dishevelled, her dress loose and in the greatest disorder, with a faultering voice, scarcely audible, she thus addressed the Baron:—O Sir Armine, Lucretia is–is–is– Here her strength failed her; and had not Conrad flew to her aid, she would have dropped upon the marble pavement.

The Baron (every nerve tremblingly possessed with fear) articulated, What, then all is discovered! Has that traitor Bernardine confessed the —— What of Lucretia?—Torture me not with this horrid suspense—What of my brother?—What confession has that villain——I did not murder—I shall go distracted—What of Lucretia?

Here a servant entered, who with woful aspect, acquainted the Baron that a part of the castle, which had long been in a tottering condition for want of repair, was by the fury of the last night's tempest so loosened from the main supporters, that, no longer in a situation to keep its position, it had just now fallen: that Helen had narrowly escaped with life, and Lucretia,— buried in the ruins, faintly interrupted the Baron. The servant shook his head, and remained silent. Then am I a wretch indeed. Oh! this is too much for human nature to support, ejaculated Sir Armine as he hurried from the hall. Helen, a little revived by the assiduous care of Conrad, was conducted, by him, to a more secure apartment in the castle than the one she had just fled from; where he left her with Alice, her allotted attendant, and went himself in search of the Baron.

Sir Armine soon convinced himself of the truth of what his domestic had related, by hastening to the spot. Part of the decayed battlement, on the south wing of the edifice, had fallen inward, and alighting on that part of the structure where his daughter slept, bore down all beneath it, and had crushed the unhappy Lucretia as she lay in bed.

Helen, whose apartment was contiguous to Lucretia's, sustained the shock: she, however, much terrified at the noise, hurried on her apparel, and, was hastening to Lucretia's chamber, but on discovering the state of it, hardly knowing whither she fled, descended into the hall, and found Sir Armine, little less alarmed than herself.

The Baron, greatly agitated, retired from the melancholy spot: a thousand painful reflections corroded his guilty breast. Now indeed, he exclaimed, is my brother sufficiently revenged; my child, my only child is torn from me! and all, all which I now possess must devolve to the hated Edgar! Never, never,— sooner would I embrace perdition than the villain, who made me what I am,—A murderer!—Oh! horrid reflection!—had he not rejected my counsel, my brother yet had lived—his obstinate refusal of my daughter's hand occasioned his father's assassination—then, shall I not be revenged?—But that traitor Bernardine will discover all—Branded with infamy I must sustain the—— Oh torture, torture!— In this manner did he continue raving, until the presence of Conrad put an end to his soliloquy, who informed him that his daughter had been released from the rubbish, and that the surgeon did not conceive

Bernardine's wounds so dangerous as he at first—— But Lucretia! interrupted Sir Armine.

Conrad shook his head and departed.

CHAPTER XXVI

Blood hath been shed ere now i'the olden time,
Ere human statute purg'd the gen'ral weal;
Ay, and since too, murders have been perform'd
Too terrible for the ear. The times have been,
That, when the brains were out, the man would die,
And there an end; but now, they rise again,
With twenty mortal murders on their crowns,
And push us from our stools. This is more strange
Than such a murder is.

SHAKESPEARE.

SEVERAL weeks elapsed, during which time every possible research was made to discover Edgar. Lucretia had been consigned to the silent tomb, Bernardine had recruited his health sufficiently to be enabled to quit his room, the south wing of the castle had been repaired, and the Baron, his most anxious hopes blighted by the death of his child, his only child, for whose future aggrandisement his brother had been assassinated; and the man, whom of all others he had the most rooted antipathy to, heir apparent to his title and estates, tortured him almost to madness.

The beauteous Helen, though Lucretia had been far from an agreeable companion; yet, nevertheless, attended her to the place of interment; and, with unfeigned sorrow, dropped the silent tear of sensibility on the sod which enveloped her cold remains.

Bernardine's illness had produced a total reversion in his principles; the many atrocities he had been accessary to, arose in such formidable array when he imagined himself upon the bed of death, as aroused his torpid faculties to that reflection which his accursed thirst for gold had formerly steeled his mind against; he viewed his past enormities with horror and remorse,

81

and secretly vowed to devote the remainder of his life, if Providence again restored him, to penitence and sorrow.

His repentance was sincere. In a few days the surgeon pronounced him out of danger; and in a short time after, Sir Armine made him a congratulatory visit on his approaching recovery, acquainting him, at the same time, of their inability to discover Edgar's retreat, and that he was then, more firmly than ever, bent upon his destruction.

Bernardine knew the safest way to secure his situation during his convalescence, and possibly privately to assist Edgar, which he was resolved upon, as some little atonement for the injury he had already done him, would be to dissemble with the Baron, and persuade him he was, as usual, solely devoted to his interest.

It was agreed between them, that the Baron should himself visit the banditti at the ruin on the forest, admonish them to continue indefatigable in their research, and that Bernardine should set out earlier on the day, and acquaint the gang of the Baron's intention.

This Bernardine agreed to, tho' secretly determined, if possible, to persuade the ruffians to abandon the pursuit; which accomplished, and Edgar freed from their machinations, to effect an escape from them himself, endeavour to procure an honest livelihood, and pass the remainder of his days in contrition for his past transgressions.

In a few days after this conference, this project was carried into execution; Bernardine quitted the castle in the morning, and though the ruin of the forest was only seven miles distant, it was nearly twilight before he arrived there; for his health being yet in a very precarious state, he was frequently necessitated to rest himself by the way; and the journey, though short, was almost too much for his enfeebled limbs to support. It had been agreed upon between himself and the Baron, as the best system they could adopt, to avoid the scrutinizing and impertinent curiosity of the residentiaries at castle Fitz-Elmar, to perform the journey on foot.

Sir Armine began his route as the dusky clouds of night began to envelope the surrounding scenery: he was met by a party of the robbers, whom Bernardine had detached to escort him; they soon arrived at their destination, and the Baron, being the first who entered the structure, on descrying the exact model of his murdered brother, clad in the same armour as when they last parted,—appalled at the sight, he would have fled, but was incapable. He retreated backward to the entrance, and fell lifeless into the arms of his escort, part of whom immediately rushed into the edifice; but on perceiving all was tranquil, again joined their confederates without, much amazed at the Baron's sudden surprize and illness.

Sir Armine they found still insensible; they attempted every possible method they were masters of to recover him, but without effect; wherefore, finding all their endeavours fruitless, they deputed Hubert, and three more of their associates, to reconduct him to the castle, deliver him into the charge of his household, and leave him to account for his sudden indisposition when again restored to reason, in whatever way he chose to adopt, as most congenial with his own ideas and feeling.

Sir Armine was conveyed to the castle as agreed, and delivered into the charge of his domestics; Helen was quickly informed of the Baron's illness, who since the demise of Lucretia, had been looked upon by the household as their mistress; and the Baron, by her attention and ready willingness to oblige him, began to soften that rigidness of conduct toward her which he had some time previous to his daughter's dissolution adopted. One circumstance, I believe, operated more forcibly in softening the austerity of Sir Armine, than all her attention to him:— Helen had received a letter from her brother, and his arrival was now hourly expected.

Helen, therefore, on being informed of the Baron's indisposition, immediately flew to his assistance, had him conveyed to bed, where he continued in the same melancholy situation until the dawn of day, when a deep drawn and heart-rending sigh, which proceeded from her patient, inspired Helen with hopes of his returning health; but, alas! how falacious are our judgments! the torpidity which had confined the Baron, as in the clay-cold grasp of death, was now succeeded by a violent delirium. Frequently would he call on his departed brother for forgiveness, acknowledge himself his assassin, and, in the fever of his mind, would dash his fists with violence on his temples, or tear the hair by handfuls from his head, until his phrenzy arrived at such an alarming height, that Helen, much terrified, ordered the domestics (as there was no other way of securing him) to fasten him with cords to the bed. The surgeon who had attended Bernardine, and who had not yet left the castle, used every effort in his power to restore him, but to no purpose; acquainted Helen, that if his disorder did not shortly take a favourable turn, he could not survive another night.

However, toward the evening he appeared a little composed, when the surgeon ordered the cords which confined him to be loosened. He seemed partly to have regained his senses, and made signs (for as yet he had not spoken) to be raised up in the bed. Helen, enraptured at the change, flew to his bed-side, and was proceeding to enquire about his health, when the door of the apartment was dashed open, and a figure (armed at all points) stalked into the room! Helen shrieked and fainted—the servants, terrified, instantly fled—and the Baron, with a yell of horror, again dropped senseless on his pillow.

CHAPTER XXVII

Ay, but to die, and go we know not where;
To lie in cold obstruction, and to rot;
This sensible warm motion to become
A kneaded clod; and the delighted spirit
To bathe in fiery floods, or to reside
In thrilling regions of thick-ribb'd ice;
To be imprison'd in the viewless winds,
And blown with restless violence round about
The pendant world; or to be worse than worst
Of those, that lawless and uncertain thoughts
Imagine howling!—'tis too horrible!
This weariest and most loath'd worldly life
That age, ach, penury, and imprisonment
Can lay on nature, is a paradise
To what we fear of death.

SHAKESPEARE.

IT is now time we should return and learn what passed at the ruin of the old castle.

On Edgar's descent into the vault, the cords with which he had been pinioned were presently unloosed, the bandage taken from his eyes, when he beheld, to his extreme joy and astonishment, his old friend Bardolph, in *propria personæ*, standing by his side.

Edgar was proceeding to interrogatories, when the affectionate old man, throwing himself at his feet, interrupted his enquiries, by exclaiming, My dear young master, you appear surprised at beholding your faithful servant at your feet; and indeed, circumstances considered, it is no more than what might naturally be expected — and then the coercive measures I was necessitated to adopt in conveying you to this spot, without disturbing the honest gentlemen who occupy the other part of this gloomy structure, must likewise tend to augment your embarrassment. But listen to my tale, and you'll find that poor

85

Bardolph, who experiences no greater pleasure than finding opportunities to succour the son of his kind benefactor, has never degenerated in principle from what you once thought him; and if he was ever worthy of being numbered amongst those with whom you could place unlimited confidence, he is still deserving of your generous friendship and attention.

Edgar, utterly unable to reply, permitted the veteran to proceed as follows:—

The night, when you, Sir, was so rudely driven from my dwelling by those honest agents of your uncle, Sir Armine Fitz-Elmar appeared little less prolific in misery to your poor servant, than the worst that could be dreaded appertaining to yourself. I had every thing to fear from the baffled designs of those inhuman monsters; particularly at a juncture when a failure of their project would have been ascribed to my officious zeal, which it was too palpable to all of them, had been exerted to promote your escape.

Wherefore, Sir, perfectly aware of my danger, I apprized my wife of my fears, and found her sentiments congenial with my own: for Dorothy, as well as myself, had distantly observed you in your flight, and was sensible of our extreme jeopardy; and as the only means of warding the destruction which seemed suspended over our heads but by the single support of a hair, which a moment's delay might to our utter ruin snap in twain, we hurried, as fast as our feeble limbs would convey us, over the dreary extent of the forest.

Towards day-break, our strength nearly exhausted, we descried the humble habitation of Hilderbrand Godfrey, an old friend of mine, who I was well acquainted had been esteemed by our late master, Sir Edgar, and would ever remain firm and unshaken in the interest of that part of the family. With him we sought a temporary refuge from present fears, and was joyfully admitted into his dwelling.

I informed him of our calamity; he sympathised in our distresses, and expressed many regrets at not having it in his power to proffer the administering hand of comfort to the son of his deceased benefactor.

His residence being only two miles distant from castle Fitz-Elmar, enabled me to observe almost every transaction there which might militate to our disadvantage, as I often have, by the most unfrequented paths gained the castle towards the close of the evening, and with intense diligence endeavoured to discover the nefarious designs that were devising there to annoy us in future.

Hilderbrand soon acquainted me of the destruction of my little property by those accursed miscreants, in revenge for their disappointment; and likewise informed me, that Bernardine, severely wounded, had been delivered into the charge of the domestics at the castle.

Here Edgar appeared much amazed, and was proceeding with many urgent enquiries, but was interrupted by Bardolph's requesting him to restrain his curiosity for the present, and listen to the sequel of his tale.

We learnt, continued Bardolph, at the expiration of a few weeks after this incident, during which time every possible means to discover your sanctuary had been used to no purpose, that Bernardine, contrary to the expectation of every one, was pronounced by the surgeon out of danger, and that in a short time we might expect to find him as great an enemy to injured innocence as he had proved himself on former occasions; but in this we were agreeably deceived: you have nothing more to dread from him. The hand of Remorse pressed heavy upon his guilty breast as he lay extended on the bed of sickness, particularly for those atrocities he had already perpetrated at the instigation of Sir Armine; and as the only means to obtain forgiveness for his past injuries to you, Sir, he endeavours, by wearing the mask of hypocrisy in the presence of your uncle, to render you secretly all the service in his power, though unknown to every person in existence, save honest Hilderbrand, who aided my efforts in conducting you hither, and your humble servant.

My kind affectionate friend, exclaimed Edgar, inform me how you wrought this wonderful change in the heart of one whom I long since imagined dead to every sense of honour and humanity.

Bernardine, continued Bardolph, as he began to recruit his strength, used frequently to stroll over the ground adjoining my friend Hilderbrand's dwelling, as its situation was more open and airy than the purlieus of the castle, and of course more salutary and conducive to his recovery. For many days successively I observed him in his melancholy peregrination, ere I could summon sufficient courage to discover myself to him.

It was then several weeks after my arrival at Hilderbrand's, during which time, Sir, notwithstanding I had used every likely method to obtain information, I could never learn where you had secreted yourself; which gave rise to a painful surmise in my mind, that the Baron must have discovered your retreat, and that you had fallen another victim to increase the catalogue of crimes already executed by the diabolical contrivances of your sanguinary uncle. The more I reflected, the more I was convinced of its probability. My situation grew irksome, and I determined, the first opportunity, to disclose myself to Bernardine, oblige the villain to inform me every thing he knew upon the subject, and rid myself of the horrid suspense which preyed upon my spirits, and was undermining my constitution.

Bernardine, I was too well acquainted, was the Baron's principal agent in all his iniquitous projects, and most probably he had confided to him every transaction that had occurred during his illness; wherefore at all events I was determined to encounter him, as the only method left me to obtain intelligence. I was at first dubious whether my threats would sufficiently intimidate him, as I was predetermined not to bend his stubborn nature to my interest by more coercive measures, and that his person should be safe from every violence my words might portend. In short, Sir, I threw myself in his way:—at the first sight of me he would have fled, but I rushed upon him, seized him by the throat, and prevented him; then furiously urged my purpose. How great was my surprize to behold him throw himself at my feet, and in broken accents, sobs almost preventing his articulation, confess his enormities, and tell me he had long wished for such an interview, to make all the atonement in his power for what he had done, and evince me of his sincere contrition by acknowledging every thing wherein you, my honoured master, was concerned. I at first conceived it entirely a stratagem to disarm me of my anger, and rudely demanded, if such had been his intention, why he endeavoured to avoid me? He replied, his astonishment was so complete at so unexpectedly beholding me; the many crimes he had suggested to encompass our ruin, all rushed with such renovated energy upon his memory, that he, without knowing what he did, strove to escape the man whom he was certain could not look upon him without horror and detestation.

Half convinced of his sincerity, I conducted him to Hilderbrand's habitation, where his extreme distress and humiliating confessions, in a short time convinced me that his contrition was beyond deceit. There it was that he laid open to me such scenes of villany as will freeze your blood to hear recited; for he informed me, that your father was—— Here a noise from above broke the thread of his discourse. The entrance into the vault was gently raised, and Hilderbrand descended, bearing the figure of the yet inanimate Bernardine.

Edgar and Bardolph immediately hastened to his assistance, seated him on the cold mould of the vault, and applied the most likely methods in their power to restore him. A short space of time convinced them that their endeavours were not without effect; his returning reason, however, was but of short duration; the wound on his temple, by his last sudden astonishment and fall burst open, and the immense quantity of blood which had issued from him in consequence, had so extremely reduced him, that his recovery seemed beyond the bounds of probability to expect.

Returning reason, however, once more revisited his debilitated frame, when fixing his haggard and sunken eye upon Bardolph, faintly pronounced, "Ah! my friend, I feel my last moments fast approaching. I feel I must die—mingle with the dust ere repentance has sealed my par—— Yet may I hope forgiveness? — Impossible! — My crimes weigh heavy on —— My hands imbrued in the blood of the innocent! — O! Bardolph, should you ever again behold that injured youth, tell him of my contri —— Tell him — You know what I would say — utterance is denied me — my blood grows chill about my heart —a heavy pressure sinks me to — Oh! my eyes wax dim. — Oh! thou great Eternal—pardon—mercy—Oh! forgive!—I come!— —Oh! mercy, mercy!"

The pulse faintly throbbed for the last time—the icy arm of Death closed for ever the mortal gates of existence, and the soul with rapid flight quitted his inanimate trunk to enter upon the dread regions of eternity.

CHAPTER XXVIII

Murder most foul, as in the best it is;
But this most foul, strange, and unnatural.
  *   *   *   *   *   *
It will have blood, they say; blood will have blood.
                                              SHAKESPEARE.

EDGAR, nearly overcome by the scene he had just witnessed, retired from the body: and Bardolph, having satisfied himself that Bernardine really was dead, joined him, where he had seated himself in a remote corner of the vault, and began as follows:—

"My dear master, if you take a retrospect of the occurrences of these last two years, you will not be surprized, when I acquaint you, that it was Bernardine and his associates, in consideration of five hundred marks, promised, and since paid to them by your incorrigible uncle, that assassinated your father within one hundred paces from the spot where we are now reclining."

My uncle? repeated Edgar, as he started from the ground—then were my forebodings but too true:—O hellish monster!—May the wrath of Heaven be showered upon my dastard head if I do not revenge——— Hold, interrupted Bardolph, make no rash asseveration—leave him to the acute reproaches of his own conscience, and doubt not but Providence will provide a punishment adequate to his crimes. Edgar wept. Bardolph used his utmost endeavours to still the tumult in his mind; which having in part accomplished, he resumed his tale, as follows:—

"After Bernardine had confessed the murder of your father, and other diabolical contrivances which had been put in practice to destroy yourself, the tenor of our discourse turned upon what means we could possibly devise and adopt to coun-

91

teract those of Sir Armine; and, if possible, prevent you again falling into his clutches. Your adventure at this place, on the night of your abdicating the castle, recurred to my recollection, and of your positive determination at some future period to revisit it. This I recapitulated to Bernardine, and requested him to solve those incidents that were envelopped in mystery to you, Sir, and had ever been an object of no less ambiguity to myself. He acquainted me, though not without much apparent compunction for his conduct, That the old ruin of the castle on the forest, for more than ten years, had been inhabited by a desperate gang of murderers; and, that he had himself been the primitive cause of their congregating on this spot; for, continued he, after I had for a series of years pursued my fortune as a footpad, in different parts of this kingdom, I at last stumbled on this mouldering structure—immediately an idea rushed into my mind, ever prolific in stratagems to annoy the public, that this place would be a most eligible situation, if a party could be convened, of the same stamp as myself, whose sole employment should be to rifle from the unwary passenger the hard earned gainings of honest industry, and apply it to our own several uses. After much perseverance, I at length succeeded beyond my most sanguine expectations:—I collected together thirty of the most desperate ruffians that ever shed blood for plunder, and took possession of the ruin I had before recommended for our future residence.

"We soon, with unremitting labour, made the edifice more convenient for our purpose, by removing some of the huge fragments of the walls, which had, by the rude shocks of the elements, been tumbled from its summit, to fill up the apertures of the decayed parts nearer to its base; and in a short time after our arrival, we had so judiciously contrived it, that not an individual could enter it but by one pass; the door to which being furnished with hidden springs, that, when shut, it would defy the utmost endeavours of every person, but those immediately in the secret (without crushing it to atoms, which would have been a work of some little difficulty) to have opened it. However, this proved of little utility; for the honest peasants, for many miles around, had been so wrought upon with the legends of the old castle, particularly of its being visited by evil spirits, and so forth, that hardly a soul had the courage to venture within a league of it after sunset; and even in the blaze of day few would willingly advance within its gloomy precincts.

"The door, which you had with much labour forced open, led to an apartment from whence the ray of light was feebly emitted, which had been appropriated for themselves to assemble and carouse in, as being one of the most remote in the mouldering edifice. Fortunately the major part of this predaceous society were absent; three of them only, on that evening, were in their council-room convened; they, on hearing such a rough salute at the door, accompanied with a voice they were utterly unacquainted with, became convulsed with fear, immediately seized the light and fled.

"Bernardine at this juncture entered the castle—was much surprized at not beholding the lamp in its accustomed situation; as it had been agreed amongst themselves, that a lamp in that apartment should be kept perpetually burning; which, only when the apprehension of detection frowned upon them, was to be extinguished, that the absentees, on their return, might have the earliest notice of their danger.

"Bernardine feared all was not right; he, with great perturbation, pursued the same passages which you had but a few seconds previously traced. In groping his way in the dark, you jostled each other; he, in his turn, became terrified and fled. Soon after, a great part of the gang returned; he informed them of his adventure; they, anxious to discover the cause of his alarm, soon procured a light: you, at the moment they were approaching toward you, providentially, ascended a staircase, and preserved your life by descending through a trap-door which lay hid in a recess nearly on its summit."

And, can you, Bardolph, explain to me how the body which—— My blood runs chill within me as I contemplate upon the horrid incidents of that eventful night!

I can, Sir. The vault into which you so fortunately alighted, was appropriated to receive the bodies of those whom this hellish crew deemed it most expedient to deprive of life before they plundered, as safer from detection than the cloysters, where rested the mouldering bones of the first inhabitants of the priory.

But, however, to resume my story, the broken door, and the removal of the lamp, two circumstances which none of the banditti could account for, became a subject of much amazement to them all: a few days however expunged it from their imaginations, and every thing was carried on as usual.

And were they never made acquainted with the particulars of that event? rejoined Edgar.—Never, replied Bardolph; nor had Bernardine the smallest idea, bordering on the truth, respecting it, until I informed him.

That some person had, in a strange manner, entered the structure, was firmly asserted by those whom you had alarmed; but who it was, or what became of him, is an enigma they have not been enabled to solve to this hour.

Bardolph then entered upon a detail of what had befallen Bernardine after Edgar had escaped from the mystical rendezvous in the wood, the death of Lucretia, and some other incidents Edgar was before not apprized of.

But my honest friend, observed Edgar, when Bardolph had finished, you have forgot to acquaint me, or is it a circumstance you have not the knowledge of, how this armour—— That can I likewise explain to you, interrupted Bardolph; it was stripped from the murdered body of your father by Bernardine, as a suit of apparel that he conceived might be of essential service to himself. To hide it from his associates, he planted it in a niche in the wall, behind a full length portrait in the hall, which first presents itself to view as you enter this immense and once magnificent fabric.

Sir Edgar, with the ruffians who perished in the affray, they left upon the spot where they fell, it being deemed by most of the banditti more politic than conveying them to the accustomed receptacle, as it would impress every person who might hereafter be informed of the assassination, that it had been perpetrated by some unknown persons, with no other motive than to possess themselves of what little property he carried about him; and Sir Armine Fitz-Elmar would escape the most distant suspicion of his having been a principal in the horrid deed.

Edgar, starting from his seat, with much effervescency exclaimed, Bardolph, I am determined this evening to appear before my uncle, accuse him with—— My dear Sir, interrupted Bardolph, pray, for once take an old friend's advice, and for the present defer so dangerous an enterprize; reflect upon the consequences of so rash an act—no good can possibly accrue—

Well, well, my good fellow, rejoined Edgar, I submit to your superior judgment, and postpone it for the present; but on some future opportunity—But, dear Bardolph, do you think it possible for me to obtain an interview with Helen, unknown to Sir Armine?—Bardolph made no reply—To-morrow night, continued Edgar, I am unchangeably resolved to attempt it.—Bardolph used his utmost endeavours to dissuade him, but without effect.

Edgar at last changed the topic, by reminding Bardolph that he had not completed his narrative; for, continued he, I am not acquainted as yet, how you became an inmate here.

I have little more to recite to you, replied Bardolph; but that, as you had declared to me your intention to revisit this ruin, I, by the advice of Bernardine, who informed me, that he could provide me with such a situation here as would not only conceal me from the scrutinizing observations of its sanguinary inhabitants, but would also afford me a distinct view of every person who entered the building, it was the only system which promised to restore you again to my sight; and even that, hardly bore a probability of its succeeding accordant to my desires; however, I closed with his proposal, and arrived here several weeks ago.

Every thing that I have heretofore had occasion for, has Bernardine abundantly supplied me with: Hilderbrand has been my companion, which has rendered my concealment less unpleasant than it otherwise must have proved. An obscure room, in the north angle of the fabric, has been our allotted residence; where we have diurnally and nocturnally been upon the watch, that no person in direction to its entrance could escape our observation.

Last night, secure as you imagined yourself, did I behold you advance; fortunately most of the robbers were absent; I quitted my hiding-place, and was hastening to disclose myself to you: ere I arrived, you had retired; and for some little time my utmost vigilance could not discover which pass you had pursued: I heard the fall of the armour, obtained a glimpse of you, just as you had fixed it upon yourself: I was rushing toward you when your uncle suddenly appeared; you fled, I followed, but could not overtake you: I witnessed your embarrassment at beholding Bernardine. Hilderbrand had observed my anxiety, pursued my steps, and soon joined me: I informed him the occasion of it; and, as the only means to avoid disturbing any individual who was not in our interest, we took advantage of your surprize, secured you by force, and bore you between us to this dreary apartment.

CHAPTER XXIX

Sure, 'tis a serious thing to die, my soul!
What a strange moment must it be, when near
Thy journey's end thou hast the gulph in view!
That awful gulph no mortal ere repass'd,
To tell what's doing on the other side.

BLAIR.

EDGAR, Bardolph, and Hilderbrand, at the conclusion of this recital removed from the vault to their watch-room, which had been assigned them by Bernardine in the north angle of the edifice; from whence Edgar sallied forth on the subsequent evening, accompanied by Bardolph and Hilderbrand, to obtain an interview, if possible, with Helen at castle Fitz-Elmar.

They soon gained the ramparts of the fabric, and began to reconnoitre: every thing appeared tranquil; the most profound silence reigned around; not a sound was heard, save the deep-toned chiming of the castle-clock, announcing the period of the night.

Edgar, perceiving all quiet, no one to obstruct his purpose, entered by a private door; here it was agreed Bardolph and Hilderbrand should keep watch, while Edgar with cautious steps endeavoured to reach Helen's apartment; but he had more difficulties to encounter than he at first imagined; for Helen, since the accident which had proved so fatal to Lucretia, had removed from the room which she had formerly occupied, and with her present retirement, Edgar was entirely unacquainted.

Several rooms, at the extreme risk of discovery, he, without meeting the object of his search, explored, when a faint murmur attracted his attention; he arrived at the door thro' which he conceived the sound had issued; he listened gently; all was silent for some time, when the noise was again renewed. Helen's

97

voice struck full upon his ear; he could not be mistaken; he placed his eye to the key-hole, and was attempting to discover if any person besides Helen was in the apartment, when his pressure against the door caused it to fly open with such sudden velocity, that he had nearly fallen prostrate upon the floor. It was his unexpected and terrific appearance, clad in complete armour, that occasioned the hurry and confusion as described in Chap. XXVI, it being his uncle's room into which he had with so much precipitancy entered.

Edgar, almost as much astonished as the terrified servants, was at first inclined to make his escape, when the distressed situation of Helen caught his eye; he lost all recollection of himself, and darted to her assistance.

Edgar, who was bestowing all his attention to restore his Helen, was quickly aroused to a sense of his own danger by the hoarse voice of the surgeon, demanding who he was, and what could have thus induced him to burst in upon their privacy.

Edgar perceiving it no longer possible to remain concealed without abandoning the object of his affection, removed the casque from his head. The surgeon immediately recognised him, and at his request hastened to the relief of Helen, who soon exhibited signs of returning life; when a hollow groan from the Baron occasioned Edgar to turn his eyes that way. The haggard countenance of his uncle, whom he had not before perceived, met his sight; much confounded, he would have interrogated the surgeon, had not the dubious state of his dear Helen prevented him.

At the particular request of the surgeon they sojourned to another apartment, gently bearing Helen between them, where she soon resumed her faculties; and the emotion of joyful surprize which the presence of Edgar excited, amply repaid for the extreme terror which had assailed her on beholding his uncouth figure when he first made his appearance.

Here an explanation took place; and Edgar learnt in part (conjecture informed him the rest) the occasion of the Baron's illness.

Old Conrad, with the major part of the household now crouded around Edgar, ashamed of their fears the first view of him had excited, and much elated at his return; for most of them had ever been attached to his interest, though to have avowed as much within hearing of Sir Armine, would have insured them instant dismission from his service.

The surgeon, who had quitted the room as Helen began to revive, re-entered, and acquainted them that the Baron, in strong convulsions had just breathed his last.

Edgar, followed by Helen, soon reached the apartment where Sir Armine lay stretched upon the couch of death; a spectacle, from the convulsive agonies of his last moments, dreadful to behold.

Edgar, on reviewing the emaciated form of his uncle, felt an emotion of pity thrill upon his heart; but when he contemplated the object before him as the murderer of his much beloved, his honoured father, the reflection was too poignant for sensibility like his to support.

With tears gushing from his eyes he hurried out of the room, and, in the anguish of his mind threw himself upon a settee which stood in the apartment he had only a few minutes previously retired from, and sobbed aloud. The conflict of the passions occasioned by the scene he had witnessed, was soon over, and he regained his wonted serenity of mind.

CHAPTER XXX

Wedlock was design'd
By gracious Heaven, to watch the mind,
To pair the tender and the just.

COTTON.

EDGAR was now the undisputed successor to castle Fitz-Elmar, together with all its appurtenances, which had formerly been his father's, or Sir Armine's; and the domestics collectively, in lieu of having the traits of sorrow depicted on their features, which the death of their old master might be expected to produce, on each face was imprinted that hilarity of thought usual when the mind is satisfied, and the heart at ease.

Bardolph and Hilderbrand, who began to wax uneasy at the long absence of Edgar, entered the fabric, and were soon apprized of the event which had detained him, by Conrad; and judging concealment no longer requisite, seated themselves before a blazing fire in the hall, till the lateness of the hour induced them, as they concluded Edgar to be in perfect safety, to sojourn to Hilderbrand's humble but happy residence.

In due time the Baron was interred, and in the cold sod that enveloped him from human observation, was buried the resentment of Edgar, though a retrospect of occurrences would engender the tear of sad remembrance in his eyes, which, not even the presence of his much adored Helen could dissipate.

A few days from the funeral had scarcely passed away, when the arrival of several attendants on horseback announced the return of Helen's brother from the continent. He had not received the letters that had been transmitted to him until several months subsequent to the demise of his father; and not expecting an event that would so immediately require his presence in England, he had been travelling for his amusement,

100

in almost every direction, over the country where he then was, having left orders at the post-office at Naples previous to his excursion, and to which place his letter had been addressed, that in case any packet should arrive, directed for him, to detain it at the office until his return: these orders unfortunately had been punctually observed.

Soon after his arrival at castle Fitz-Elmar, did Edgar, to the great satisfaction of all parties, conduct the blooming Helen to the altar. Time, instead of diminishing, increased their affections;—their loves had been founded on the basis of Virtue, and Hymen fast rivetted them in the fetters of Contentment.

A short space of time had elapsed from their nuptials, when Edgar, with the intention of surprising and bringing to condign punishment the banditti who infested the ruins of the old castle, summoned together his vassals, and surrounded the structure, but the villains were fled; they, finding their retreat discovered, anticipated what would happen, soon abdicated the building, dispersed themselves over different parts of the country, and pursued, separately, their hellish avocations, until detection conducted them to the tree of Justice, where they received the reward their many atrocities so richly entitled them to expect.

Bernardine, together with several others whom they discovered there, and at their secret rendezvous in the wood, they had decently interred; and peace and tranquillity once more reigned throughout the vicinity of castle Fitz-Elmar.

Bardolph, and his hospitable wife Dorothy, spent the remainder of their days at the castle, happy in contemplating the felicity of their honoured master.

Helen's brother married a lady of good family and large fortune; had a large mansion built in the neighbourhood, and long partook of the hilarity which prevailed at castle Fitz-Elmar, and diffused itself miles around.

Edgar was blest with a numerous progeny, and, in the danger he had escaped, proved that the efforts of an honest mind, though poor and unprotected, will eventually rise superior to the deep-laid machinations of vice, though armed with wealth and power; for Providence will safely guide him through the thorny labyrinths of affliction in this world, and into happiness eternal in the world to come.

> The man who consecrates his hours
> By vig'rous effort, and an honest aim,
> At once he draws the sting of life and death;
> He walks with Nature, and her paths are peace.
> DR. YOUNG.

THE END

NOTES

Page

1 **"conscious that I never wrote a line..."** Susanna Rowson, *Mentoria, or the Young Ladies' Friend* (1794).

3 **epigraph:** Robert Blair, "The Grave" (1743). Blair was among the most important of the "Graveyard Poets," a school of poets which also included Thomas Gray and Edward Young, and whose poems often focused on the subject of human mortality. The works of these poets were extremely influential on early Gothic writers.
"The lightning flash'd in vivid colours, and the thunder rolled in awful majesty.": I have been unable to trace this quotation.
"When Edgar, who almost exhausted...": This strange construction, with the preceding sentence concluding with a comma, and the new paragraph commencing with a fragment, is Sickelmore's, and has been printed here exactly as in the first edition.

4 **banditti:** Italian for "bandits"; Sickelmore, like most Gothic writers, uses "banditti" as both a singular and a plural noun.

8 **epigraph:** Shakespeare, *Hamlet*, III, ii. The second line is misquoted, and should read, "The hart ungall'd go play"
Bardolph: Shakespeare's influence on Sickelmore is evident in the naming of the characters. Edgar is a character in *King Lear*, Bardolph figures in *Henry IV, Henry V,* and *The Merry Wives of Windsor*, and Bernardine, introduced later, appears in *Measure for Measure* (spelled Barnardine in Shakespeare's play).

9 **Morpheus:** the Greek god of sleep.

11 **epigraph:** Aaron Hill, *Zara* (1736), V, i.

12 **lowring:** lowering, appearing dark and threatening.

13 **obsecration:** beseeching or imploring the assistance of God.

15 **The fellow pretended to be satisfied with this answer:** Sickelmore frequently, and somewhat clumsily, foreshadows future events in the plot. As will be seen later in the story, Bernardine is not satisfied with the answer.

16 **epigraphs:** the first is from *The Day of Judgment: a Poetical Essay* (1758) by Dr. Robert Glynn, the second is from Shakespeare's *Twelfth Night*, III, ii.

17 **"Her face most filthy was to see..."**: Edmund Spenser, *The Faerie Queene*, Book 4, Canto I.

18 **epigraph**: Shakespeare, *Julius Caesar*, V, v.
"An eye like Mars...": Shakespeare, *Hamlet*, III, iv.
Knight-Banneret: a knight specially honoured for valour. The knight-banneret was a rank higher than knight-bachelor, and lower than baron. Knights-banneret were entitled to lead troops under their own banner.

20 **epigraph**: William Havard, *Regulus*, II, vii.
"Hope left the heart...": An expanded version of this quotation occurs in Ann Yeardsley's *The Royal Captives* (1795), unattributed there as here. I have been unable to determine if Yeardsley was quoting from an earlier source, or if she is the author of the lines.

23 **epigraph**: Robert Blair, "The Grave"

24 **sanguifluous**: flowing or running with blood.

26 **epigraph**: Nicholas Rowe, *The Tragedy of Jane Shore* (1714), II, i.
carbuncles: painful sores on the skin with holes for the discharge of pus.

28 **"horror struck upon his heart"**: Ann Radcliffe, *The Romance of the Forest* (1791).

29 **epigraph**: Shakespeare, *Macbeth*, V, v.
"his silver skin lac'd": *Macbeth*, II, iii.

32 **epigraph**: a passage frequently quoted by Gothic novelists, the lines are from the "Celadon and Amelia" episode of the "Summer" part of James Thomson's *The Seasons* (1727). Thomson's *Seasons* was extraordinarily influential on the Gothic writers, particularly Ann Radcliffe, who quotes it repeatedly in *The Mysteries of Udolpho* (1794).
epocha: variant of epoch, meaning "a particular period of history."

33 **"her form was fresher..."**: from the "Palemon and Lavinia" episode in James Thomson's *The Seasons*.
"unconscious of her pow'r": also from the "Palemon and Lavinia" episode of Thomson's *Seasons*.

35 **facinorous**: extremely wicked

36 **epigraph**: Shakespeare, *Cymbeline*, III, vi.

39 **epigraph**: Shakespeare, *Macbeth*, III, ii.

43 **epigraph:** *Macbeth*, II, i.

44 **a hermit:** Hermits figure in a great number of Gothic novels. Compare Sickelmore's hermit with the hermits in John Palmer's *The Mystery of the Black Tower* (1796) and Francis Lathom's *The Midnight Bell* (1798).

45 **epigraph:** John Pomfret, "Cruelty and Lust" (1699).
    sans ceremonie: French for "without ceremony".

47 **epigraph:** Joseph Addison, *Cato* (1713), I, i.
    "Descended from an indigent family…": another of Sickelmore's fragments.
    Hymen: Greek god of marriage.
    angels: gold coins current in Britain from the mid 1400s through the mid 1600s, so called because they bore the image of the archangel Michael.

48 **marks:** an obsolete monetary unit in medieval England and Scotland.

50 **obduce:** to draw over, as a covering.

52 **epigraph:** This quotation may be from one of the many works by the prolific writer Samuel Jackson Pratt (1749-1814), but I have been unable to trace it.
    anchorite: someone who has retired into seclusion for religious reasons.
    "Man soon tires of everything…": Voltaire, *Candide* (1759)

55 **epigraph:** *Macbeth*, III, ii.

56 **irresolute and undetermined:** attributes usually associated with Hamlet, and one of many indications in the text that the character of Edgar is based on that of Hamlet.

58 **epigraph:** Horace Walpole, *The Mysterious Mother* (1768). This reference, like the quote from Radcliffe earlier in the novel, is intended to acknowledge Sickelmore's debt to Walpole and Radcliffe, two of the most celebrated Gothic novelists.

59 **mucid:** moldy and slimy

60 **casque:** helmet

61 **epigraph:** Robert Blair, "The Grave"

63 **epigraph:** *King John*, III, ii.

65 **epigraph:** *Titus Andronicus*, V, i.

66 **lucrific:** profitable

105

68 **epigraph**: Thomas Goffe, *The Raging Turk* (1618).

71 **epigraph**: *Macbeth*, V, v.

74 **tumbled her withered trunk into the pit**: This graphic description of Black Mary's murder is one of a few passages in the book that lead one to believe Sickelmore's preface, in which he disclaims any intention of conveying "wrong ideas" or "corrupt[ing]" his readers, is somewhat disingenuous.

75 **epigraph**: *Romeo and Juliet*, V, iii.

76 **shake not your gory locks at me**: *Macbeth*, III, iv.

78 **epigraph**: *Macbeth*, IV, iii.

79 **crushed the unhappy Lucretia**: this recalls the crushing of the usurper's similarly unpleasant offspring in *The Castle of Otranto* (1764). In *Otranto*, Manfred's son Conrad is crushed beneath a gigantic helmet.

81 **epigraph**: *Macbeth*, III, iv. In the first edition of *Edgar; or, the Phantom of the Castle*, the second line reads "Ere human statue…"; I have changed "statue" to "statute", as "statue" does not make sense and is not the word used in Shakespeare's original. Most editions of *Macbeth* read: "Ere human statute purg'd the gentle weal", but I have not changed "gen'ral" to "gentle," as it appears to be Sickelmore's, not his printer's, error.

85 **epigraph**: *Measure for Measure*, III, i.

91 **epigraph**: *Hamlet*, I, v. and *Macbeth*, III, iv.

97 **epigraph**: Robert Blair, "The Grave".

99 **the baron had just breathed his last**: Sir Armine's death is extremely anticlimactic and must have been unsatisfying to readers of the day, who had come to expect some appropriate punishment for the Gothic villain.

100 **epigraph**: Nathaniel Cotton, "Marriage", from *Visions in Verse* (1760).

102 **"The man who consecrates his hours…"**: Edward Young, *The Complaint: or Night Thoughts on Life, Death, and Immortality* (1741).

APPENDIX

CONTEMPORARY REVIEWS OF
EDGAR; OR, THE PHANTOM OF THE CASTLE

*Edgar: or the Phantom of the Castle. A Novel. In Two Vols.
By R. Sicklemore.* 12mo. 7s. Lane. 1798.

Although we cannot assign a very high rank to this production, we do not think it contemptible; and it will afford some entertainment to the *amateurs* of horror. It was written for a benevolent and useful purpose; and its moral is, that the efforts of an honest mind, though poor and unprotected, will ultimately rise superior to the deep-laid machinations of vice, though armed with wealth and power.

—— *Critical Review*, August 1798, page 473.

Edgar, or the Phantom of the Castle, a Novel. By R. Sicklemore.
7s. 12mo. Lane. 1798.

NOTWITHSTANDING Mr. R. Sicklemore falls under the censure of Horace, as one of the *servum pecus*, he may be allowed to possess the merit of *imitating*, more successfully than the generality of his brother-writers, the manner of a lady so deservedly popular as Mrs. Radcliffe.

—— *The Monthly Mirror*, September 1798, page 261

Gothic Classics

NOW AVAILABLE

THE ANIMATED SKELETON, Anonymous
128 pp. March 2005 0-9766048-0-9, $12.95

THE CAVERN OF DEATH, Anonymous (Ed. Allen Grove)
104 pp. July 2005 0-9766048-3-3, $12.95

THE CASTLE OF OLLADA by Francis Lathom
192 pp. March 2005 0-9766048-2-5, $14.95

ITALIAN MYSTERIES by Francis Lathom
350 pp. June 2005 0-9766048-6-8, $16.95

MYSTERY OF THE BLACK TOWER by John Palmer, Jun.
200 pp. July 2005 0-9766048-1-7, $14.95

THE PHANTOM OF THE CASTLE by Richard Sickelmore
128 pp. June 2005 0-9766048-9-2, $13.95

COMING SOON

WHO'S THE MURDERER? by Eleanor Sleath
700 pp. December 2005 0-9766048-8-4, $18.95

ETHELWINA by T. J. Horsley Curties
400 pp. December 2005 0-9766048-7-6, $16.95

All titles can be ordered at www.valancourtbooks.com or from
any fine local or online bookseller.

Valancourt Books, P.O. Box 220511, Chicago, IL 60622
http://www.valancourtbooks.com   gothic@valancourtbooks.com

www.ingramcontent.com/pod-product-compliance
Lightning Source LLC
Chambersburg PA
CBHW010834250626
47157CB00010B/3279